"Our appliances have until midnight next Friday to meet the hours-worked requirement, or *we'll* be in breach of contract!" Sighing, Zelda picked up her coffee mug.

"So we have to actually *use* them? Like in cook and clean the mortal way for a week?" Pouting when Aunt Zelda nodded, Sabrina picked up the charred letter that had just arrived via the toaster. "This is one of the downsides of being a witch that nobody ever talks about, right?"

"Right." Sighing, Hilda sipped her coffee. "Well, I suppose it could be worse. It could be our turn to host the monthly meeting of the Witches Living in the Mortal Realm Support Group."

"Uh-oh." Sabrina scanned the note in her hand. "Aunt Vesta's dropping by this afternoon to discuss a 'family emergency with potentially disastrous domestic consequences for all.' Quote, unquote."

Zelda and Hilda exchanged a quick glance, then abruptly stood up.

"You start on the dishes, Hilda. I'll tackle the living room."

Sabrina, the Teenage Witch™ books

#1 Sabrina, the Teenage Witch
#2 Showdown at the Mall
#3 Good Switch, Bad Switch
#4 Halloween Havoc
#5 Santa's Little Helper
#6 Ben There, Done That
#7 All You Need Is a Love Spell
#8 Salem on Trial
#9 A Dog's Life
#10 Lotsa Luck
#11 Prisoner of Cabin 13
#12 All That Glitters
#13 Go Fetch!
#14 Spying Eyes
    Sabrina Goes to Rome
#15 Harvest Moon
#16 Now You See Her, Now You Don't
#17 Eight Spells a Week (Super Edition)
#18 I'll Zap Manhattan
#19 Shamrock Shenanigans
#20 Age of Aquariums
#21 Prom Time
#22 Witchopoly
#23 Bridal Bedlam

Available from ARCHWAY Paperbacks

Sabrina The Teenage Witch™

Bridal Bedlam

Diana G. Gallagher

Based on Characters Appearing in Archie Comics

And based upon the television series
Sabrina, The Teenage Witch
Created for television by Nell Scovell
Developed for television by Jonathan Schmock

AN ARCHWAY PAPERBACK
Published by POCKET BOOKS
New York London Toronto Sydney Tokyo Singapore

AN ARCHWAY PAPERBACK *Original*

 An Archway Paperback published by
POCKET BOOKS, a division of Simon & Schuster Inc.
1230 Avenue of the Americas, New York, NY 10020

ISBN: 0-671-02818-9

First Archway Paperback printing June 1999

10 9 8 7 6 5 4 3 2 1

AN ARCHWAY PAPERBACK and colophon are registered trademarks of Simon & Schuster, Inc.

SABRINA THE TEENAGE WITCH and all related titles, logos and characters are trademarks of Archie Comics Publications, Inc.

Printed in the U.S.A.

IL: 4+

*With gratitude and affection
for my agent, Ricia Mainhardt,
and A. J.,
her happily-ever-after true love*

Chapter 1

☆

Bleary-eyed, Sabrina Spellman stumbled into the kitchen. Last night she had played foosball at the Slicery with Harvey and Val until closing, then watched a horror video at Harvey's house. Granted, popping home after two A.M. had been pushing the curfew envelope, but her aunts had been asleep and probably hadn't noticed. Besides, there were only so many Friday nights and sleep-late, do-nothing Saturday mornings in a teenager's life. The fun binge had definitely been worth the risk of annoyed guardian reprisal.

"You've got mail!" Salem announced brightly. Sprawled on the central counter, the sleek black cat stretched with a satisfied groan.

"Is it that late?" Sabrina stopped short and yawned. The mail didn't usually arrive until noon. She didn't see any letters stacked on the table by

Aunt Zelda's laptop, and the computer screen was dark, but an acrid odor wafted past her nostrils. "Something's burning!"

"I figure you've got about five seconds to take delivery before the message self-destructs," Salem said dryly.

"Oh, boy! How come the toaster didn't *ding?*" Sabrina leaped toward the smoking toaster, which doubled as the Other Realm Postal Delivery System, and hit the release lever. An envelope with charred edges popped up and burst into flame.

"Hot mail!" Salem jumped back as Sabrina doused the fire with a quick point, then flipped the smoldering letter onto the counter. He sniffed the burned paper from a safe six inches. "Smells like bad news."

"Where's the fire!" Aunt Hilda raced through the door holding a fire extinguisher. Her hair was disheveled and her open bathrobe flapped as she put on the brakes and slid across the floor.

"Looks like somebody lit one under you!" Salem chuckled.

"Are you cooking again, Hilda?" Zelda paused in the door and waved her hand in front of her face to clear the gray haze.

"It's okay." Sabrina patted the blackened envelope with a pot holder. "T-mail crashed and burned, though."

Clutching her chest, Hilda slumped into a chair. The fire extinguisher hit the floor with a thud.

"You'd think after three hundred years I'd get over my fire phobia."

"No witch ever gets over fear of fire." Zelda sank into another chair with a heavy sigh. "It's a self-preservation thing."

"Speaking of self-preservation, the cat's hungry." Salem sat down and stared at his food dish, his tail twitching.

Leaning against the counter, Sabrina absently glanced around as she fanned the still smoking but cooling letter. The kitchen, like the rest of the house, was a disaster. They had all been too busy the past week to pay much attention. Aunt Zelda was compiling the scientific research she had accumulated over the past century into a reference book she hoped to have published. Aunt Hilda had started *War and Peace* again. After eighty-nine attempts, she was determined to finish it this time. Sabrina was a teenager. Housework was not on her list of things to do under any circumstances.

"Any time," Salem snapped impatiently.

"Sorry, Salem. Coffee before kibble." Hilda raised her hand to start the coffeemaker brewing.

"Who said anything about kibble?" Salem bristled indignantly.

"I'll settle for instant this morning, Hilda," Zelda said.

"Good idea. Magic Mocha or Cauldron Chocolate?"

"I don't know." Zelda frowned thoughtfully, tapping her chin. "I rather like wizard walnut."

3

"Meanwhile," Salem drawled, "the starving cat files a complaint with the Other Realm Familiar Humane Society. Inspectors invade. Citations are written. Fines are levied—"

"All right, Salem! I'll get it." Rolling her eyes, Sabrina pulled a cat-food tin from the cupboard with a lazy point. Being hauled before the Witches' Council for familiar neglect was not how she wanted to spend the day. She flicked her finger to pop the cat-food top, but nothing happened.

"Or Swiss Witch." Hilda's finger dangled limply.

Zelda brightened. "With nutmeg?"

"This is a joke, right?" Salem eyed Sabrina narrowly. "Or is your finger on the fritz?"

"My finger was okay a second ago!" Scowling, Sabrina pointed at the can. It rose into the air and obediently zipped into her hand. Relieved, she grabbed the pop-top tab to pull. Simultaneously the electric can opener by Salem's dish raised its blade mechanism and whirred. Taking the hint, Sabrina slipped the tin under the blade and pressed down.

Salem collapsed with relief as the can opener removed the lid. "Don't bother with a spoon. Just dump it."

Sabrina upended the can into Salem's bowl and yanked her hand back as the ravenous cat dived in. She tossed the tin into the trash, then cautiously picked up the burned letter by a corner and blew on it. Bits of charred envelope drifted away, but the letter inside it was only slightly singed.

"Swiss Witch with nutmeg it is." Hilda flicked

4

her finger at the table. Two *empty* mugs appeared. "That's not what I ordered."

Sabrina started as the trash compactor door banged open and closed.

"Here, let me try." Zelda aimed her finger at the mugs.

> *"Instant Swiss Witch coffee, please,*
> *with a pinch of nutmeg seed."*

Hilda peered into the mugs. They were still empty. "Instant nothing? This isn't Say No to Caffeine Day or something equally annoying, is it?"

"Not that I'm aware of." Distressed, Zelda glanced at her finger, then aimed at the coffeemaker on the counter.

> *"Boil, bubble, toil and trouble,*
> *brew a pot of coffee—hot."*

Hilda arched an eyebrow as the coffeemaker gurgled and steaming, dark coffee started dripping through the basket into the glass pot. She turned as the trash compactor door banged open and closed again. "Is it just me or do you get the feeling that something isn't quite right here?"

"It's not just you, Aunt Hilda. The trash compactor is *really* upset."

"Maybe it wants some trash," Zelda said absently.

"Of course! I'd better feed it before *it* lodges a complaint with the Department of Abused Appliances." Dropping the letter on the table, Sabrina retrieved the cat tin from the trash basket and tossed it through the compactor's open door. A definitive *clank* sounded as the door banged closed. It immediately opened again. Sabrina whipped the lid off the can opener magnet and threw that in. "Chew it this time!"

"I don't think there is a Department of Abused Appliances." Rising, Hilda took the empty mugs to the counter. Even though the coffeemaker was only halfway through the brewing process, she pulled the pot off the warmer and poured. Coffee continued to drip through the basket and sputtered as it hit the warming plate.

"No, I don't think—mail!" Zelda jumped up as the toaster began to smoke. She hit the release button, then gingerly pulled the pop-up paper from the slot and opened it. "But apparently our appliances *do* have a 'work incentive clause' written into their purchase agreements."

"What about a 'failure to work properly' clause?" Hilda asked. "This thing is supposed to stop dripping when I pick the pot up, isn't it?" The puddle of dark liquid on the hot plate sizzled when she put the pot back.

Nodding, Zelda dropped back into her chair and kept reading.

"Maybe it's still under warranty." Sliding into another chair, Sabrina tried to point up some hot chocolate. A mug and a packet of instant cocoa mix appeared. "Okay, what's going on? I seem to have a minor magic finger malfunction."

"It's not your finger, Sabrina!" Zelda looked up in shock. "Our appliances got a Witches' Council injunction against us!"

"Injunction?" Hilda set one of the mugs in front of Zelda and sat down. "For what? We hardly ever make them work!"

"That's the problem!" Zelda dropped the court order. "The Witches' Council has suspended all our instant cleaning and cooking spells until our appliances accumulate enough annual work hours to qualify for a luxury overhaul at the Mars Mechanical Maintenance Resort!"

"You're not serious, are you?" Hilda asked.

Sabrina stared at the cocoa packet. "I'm not sure I remember *how* to boil water."

Salem licked the last speck of Pretty Kitty Salmon Delight from his bowl. "Does this mean we have to keep the can opener busy?"

"Very serious." Sighing, Zelda picked up her coffee mug. "Our appliances have until midnight next Friday to meet the hours-worked requirement."

"And if they don't?" Hilda winced as she glanced around the kitchen. Dirty dishes filled the sink and a pile of unwashed clothes spilled out the laundry room door.

"If they don't, then we'll be in breach of contract." Zelda looked at Hilda and Sabrina pointedly. "Then they can go on strike indefinitely or opt to be repossessed."

"So we have to actually *use* them? Like in cook and clean the mortal way for a week?" Pouting when Aunt Zelda nodded, Sabrina picked up the charred letter. "This is one of the downsides of being a witch that nobody ever talks about, right?"

"Right." Sighing, Hilda sipped her coffee. "Well, I suppose it could be worse. It could be our turn to host the monthly meeting of the Witches Living in the Mortal Realm Support Group."

"Uh-oh." Sabrina scanned the singed note again to make sure she had read it correctly. "Aunt Vesta's dropping by this afternoon to discuss a 'family emergency with potentially disastrous domestic consequences for all.' Quote, unquote."

Zelda and Hilda exchanged a quick glance, then abruptly stood up.

"You start on the dishes, Hilda. I'll tackle the living room."

"Me? Dishes?" Hilda glanced at the dishwasher they had recently purchased to keep up appearances. Mortal dinner guests almost always offered to help clean up.

Zelda looked back when she reached the doorway. "Sabrina. Laundry!"

"But—" Sabrina protested. She had planned to spend the day doing nothing more strenuous than trying to decide whether to catch a movie or hang out at the Slicery with Harvey and Val again that night. "Since when does Aunt Vesta care if our house is clean? Isn't a potential family disaster more important?"

"Vesta's idea of a domestic disaster is breaking a nail and not being able to match her polish spell exactly." Hilda rolled up her sleeves. "Our definition is having to spend *another* century defending our decision to live in the mortal world!"

"Vesta simply doesn't understand the satisfaction of achieving *anything* the hard way," Zelda said.

"Meaning the mortal way," Sabrina clarified.

Zelda swept her arm across the kitchen. "And if Vesta sees *this* domestic disaster, we'll *never* hear the end of it."

"It's a little hard to defend doing things the hard way when our appliances have taken legal action because we've been using magic for routine chores." Hilda's gaze zeroed in on the dishwasher.

Good point, Sabrina thought. Her flamboyant Aunt Vesta didn't realize that life in the Other Realm, where everything was possible with a flick of a finger, was boring. Although laundry wasn't exactly exciting, doing it supported the arguments in favor of leading a mortal life. Not that Aunt Vesta would ever approve or understand. Why would any self-respecting witch want to work if she didn't have to?

Good question!

At the moment, though, Sabrina and her aunts didn't have the luxury of choosing between mortal drudgery and magic.

"Does anyone have a clue how the washing machine works?" Sabrina hated to admit it, but she had gotten used to using magic for anything that remotely resembled housework, too.

"How hard can it be?" Assigned to do dishes, Hilda cautiously opened the dishwasher and peered inside. "Did this thing come with a technical manual?"

"Just stuff the clothes in, Sabrina. Then add detergent and set the dial," Zelda explained patiently. "It's automatic after that."

"Stuffing, dialing, sorting, and folding are not my idea of automatic." Grumbling, Sabrina gathered up the clothes outside the laundry room door.

Hilda pointed a dirty plate from the sink into the dishwasher rack. "I hate doing dishes by hand!"

☆

Chapter 2

☆

Help!" Sabrina called out in frustration. After three hours and four loads of trial and error, she had finally figured out the elements of basic laundry. She could measure detergent, change cycles, avoid static cling, and find enough hangers like a seasoned domestic engineer. However, there was no way to fold a fitted bottom sheet neatly.

"What?" Exasperated, Hilda stepped into the laundry room doorway and blew wisps of flyaway hair out of her eyes. Her rumpled sweats were streaked with dirt. Turning off a whirring, hand-held mini-vac, she sagged against the doorjamb.

Sabrina glanced at the pile of bed linens at her feet. "I could use some help folding these."

"Okay." Hilda flicked her finger.

The sheets rose in the air, folded themselves into

perfect squares and stacked themselves in a laundry basket.

"How come your magic worked?" Sabrina asked, pouting.

"Because we don't have a *machine* that folds clothes." Hilda glared at the mini-vac. "I wish I could say the same about dust!"

"You could have told me there was a loophole in the injunction!" Sabrina glanced at the stacks of clothes she had painstakingly sorted and folded, then looked at her finger. They didn't have a put-the-clothes-away appliance, either. She pointed, and the piles obediently floated single file out of the laundry room to put themselves into closets and drawers. "The joys of household maintenance are vastly overrated."

"Which explains why nobody's ever written a book about it." Hilda exhaled wearily.

Nodding, Sabrina pointed again and a dozen dirty towels leaped off the floor into the washer. "So—how bad do you think Aunt Vesta's family emergency is? I mean, it must be serious for her to warn us that she's coming over rather than just popping in unannounced."

"Well, unless her magic license has been revoked for exceeding the twenty-four hours a day party limit and she wants to move in with us—"

Sabrina flinched. A dozen potential disaster scenarios had gone through her mind, ranging from being stuck with her awful witch license photo for life to finding out the Spellmans had a hereditary susceptibility to spell dyslexia. Dealing with a magically grounded Aunt Vesta would be far worse.

"—it's probably nothing worse than a bunion, one of the first physical signs that witches grow old, too. Eventually."

One of the towels miscalculated its trajectory and flipped to correct its course into the washer. A terry-cloth corner snapped, knocking a box of powdered laundry detergent off the shelf. As Sabrina reached for the dustpan and brush, the mini-vac turned itself on, sprang out of Hilda's hand, and attacked the white granules spilled on the floor.

"Grab it!" Frantic, Hilda lunged for the small vacuum cleaner and closed her hand around the handle.

"Why?" Sabrina asked, bewildered. "It's just doing its job."

"Why?" Dropping to her knees, Hilda gritted her teeth and clamped her other hand on the handle. She pulled but couldn't stop the mini-vac from scoffing up the last sprinkles of white soap powder, then tearing through the top of the detergent box. "Because it doesn't know when to quit, that's why!"

Sabrina hesitated as the little machine devoured the detergent in the box, then started on the box. She grabbed the end of the box and pulled. Grunting, Hilda pulled in the opposite direction, but the ravenous mini-vac wouldn't let go.

"Watch your fingers, Sabrina!"

Finger! Sabrina released the crushed box and pointed, but the mini-vac kept running until the last bit of cardboard disappeared up its nozzle. Then it stopped and coughed up a few bits of shredded box and detergent.

"See what happens when you eat too fast!" Sabrina said.

The mini-vac burped.

Hilda collapsed against the washing machine, then jumped back as it suddenly started shaking.

"All right!" Sabrina set the dial and pulled the knob to start water flowing into the drum. "Sorry, but we're out of detergent."

"No, we're not." Hilda held the mini-vac over the washer and opened the back of the canister.

"Aunt Hilda!" Sabrina grimaced as Hilda poured a mixture of detergent and dirt into the washer.

"It's a washer, isn't it?" Hilda moved the mini-vac to a wastepaper basket and dumped the rest of the dusty debris. "So it'll wash the dirt away—"

"Yeooooow!" Salem screeched.

"Sounds like he slammed his tail in the cabinet door again." Shaking her head, Hilda moved into the kitchen.

Sabrina closed the washer lid and stepped through the door as Salem leaped toward the counter to escape the bizarre machine that was chasing him. She had never seen the contraption before. With a leather harness attached to a metal base, it rolled on round casters and resembled a mini-moon rover. A jointed, robotlike arm with a pincer claw emerged from a storage compartment under the metal plate, extended itself, and latched on to the cat's tail.

"It's got me! Help!" Salem's claws dug grooves in the cabinet as the machine pulled him down.

"Don't panic!" Dropping the mini-vac, Hilda ran to the cat's rescue. She grabbed the robot arm and pressed a button, releasing the pincer's hold. Salem immediately scrambled to safety and whirled to hiss at his attacker. Hilda waved her hands at the machine. "Shoo!"

The machine hesitated, waving its pincer arm and dropping black cat hairs on the floor. The mini-vac immediately sprang into action to clean them up, then chased the strange contraption into the dining room, sucking up the cat hairs that trailed behind it.

"What was that?" Sabrina asked.

"That's what *I'd* like to know!" The fur on Salem's arched back stood on end.

"It's an automatic cat groomer some guy was selling linen closet to linen closet." Hilda shrugged sheepishly. "It's been stashed under my bed for two years."

"I already *have* a perfectly good cat groomer!" Salem stuck out his tongue and gave his paw a couple of quick licks. "See!"

"The salesman was a hunk, huh?" Sabrina asked pointedly.

"Major hunk." Hilda sighed wistfully, then frowned. "But I never saw him again."

"Hey!" Aunt Zelda shouted from the living room. "Bring that back!"

"Now what?" Hilda threw up her hands and dashed through the door.

"Coming?" Sabrina asked Salem.

"No way!" Salem shuddered. "Not while that cat-cleaning machine is prowling the halls. I'll just wait here and suffer with unsatisfied curiosity."

"Look out, Hilda!" Zelda shouted again. "It's behind you!"

Hilda yelped in surprise.

The sound of a TV commercial increased in volume to compete with a Hootie and the Blowfish CD blaring on the stereo.

"Think I'll satisfy mine." Sabrina ran for the living room and skidded to a halt in the middle of chaos.

Piano keys plinked as the mini-vac raced across the keyboard to cut off the cat groomer's escape up the drapes. The flower arrangement on top of the piano toppled as the mini-vac zoomed by. Using its pincer arm, the cat groomer climbed to safety on the curtain rod when the mini-vac paused to suck up spilled bits of dry moss.

Looking like two mechanical bulls preparing to charge, the vacuum cleaner was faced off against the water-filled carpet shampooer on opposite sides of a pile of dirt.

"Shoo! Get!" Aunt Hilda batted at a hair dryer buzzing around her head.

"Let go!" Backed into a corner, Aunt Zelda shook her foot, trying to dislodge an automatic shoeshine machine. Her sneaker shoelace was wrapped around its bristled brush roller.

The remote controls raised the volume on the TV and CD player to decibel levels not even Sabrina's teenage ears could tolerate. She grabbed the remotes off the coffee table and pressed the mute buttons.

The sudden silence made everyone and everything pause.

And the linen closet boomed.

Two seconds later Aunt Vesta popped downstairs. As usual, Sabrina's statuesque aunt was impeccably groomed and dressed. Wearing a classic eggshell-white cashmere sweater with elegant charcoal-gray slacks and black ankle boots, she took the scene in with a sweeping glance as chaos resumed.

Taking advantage of the distraction, the vacuum cleaner suddenly swooped in, inhaled the pile of dirt and fled into the study. Not to be outdone, the carpet cleaner began shampooing the stained spot left behind. The mini-vac latched on to the drapes with its suction nozzle. The cat groomer scrambled along the rod and down the far panel to the floor, then zipped back toward the kitchen.

"This is just *too* deliciously domestic!" Aunt Vesta grinned, which surprised Sabrina. Her dazzling aunt didn't look as if she had dire family news to discuss.

"I could do without the sarcasm." Hilda grabbed the hair dryer hovering by her ear and flicked the Off switch.

"Is it afternoon already? Time really *does* fly when you're having fun." Laughing lamely, Zelda dragged the shoeshine machine into the foyer, slipped out of her sneakers and shoved the machine with her attached shoe into the closet.

"Yes, it does, doesn't it?" Vesta smiled wistfully.

"Okay, Aunt Vesta. Out with it. I can't stand the suspense!"

"Hmmmm?" Vesta looked at Sabrina blankly.

The dryer buzzer buzzed.

"Not now!" Sabrina pointed to reset the cycle to fluff, then pressed her strangely spaced-out aunt. "What's the emergency? Are we banned from Mars? Cursed with creeping crone syndrome or what?"

"I'm a little curious myself." Aunt Zelda herded the carpet shampooer into the dining room and sank onto the couch.

"Well—" Biting her lower lip, Vesta averted her gaze. "I'm not sure where to begin."

"Just blurt it out, Vesta." Hilda shut the hair dryer in a drawer and pulled the mini-vac off the drapes.

Sabrina tensed. Compared to the string of zany Spellman relatives she had met the past year, her gorgeous, poised, and totally self-indulgent Aunt Vesta was relatively normal. Watching her shift from being blissfully preoccupied one minute to being nervously anxious the next was unsettling.

"Well"—Aunt Vesta took a deep breath and smiled tightly—"I'm getting married—"

Zelda's mouth fell open.

Hilda frowned.

Sabrina grinned, relieved, delighted, and surprised—until Aunt Vesta finished her announcement.

"—to a mortal."

Chapter 3

Sabrina sat at the kitchen table with Hilda and Zelda, watching Aunt Vesta with a mixture of trepidation and curiosity. They were sipping mint tea and waiting impatiently for the free-spirited Vesta to explain. Aunt Zelda had convinced the household appliances to take a break, and the silence augmented the tension.

"I ran into Ashton on the Vermont ski slopes ten days ago." Vesta continued to stare off into space with a dreamy smile.

"Ran into him?" Sabrina cocked her head. "As in collision?"

Vesta blushed. "Deliberately."

Zelda frowned skeptically. "You've only known him for ten days?"

"That's an all-time record for someone whose

romantic interest span is usually measured in hours." Hilda blew on her steaming tea.

"It was love at first sight," Vesta gushed. "Besides, sometimes you just have to seize the moment and go for it."

Curled up on the counter, Salem opened one eye. "Not that you're prone to acting on impulse or anything."

Vesta ignored him.

"He's that handsome, huh?" Hilda scowled.

"Incredibly dashing and oozing with charm." Sighing like a smitten schoolgirl, Vesta pointed up a plate of cheese-and-cracker snacks shaped like hearts.

"Figures." Hilda's facial features wrinkled into a petulant pout and her complexion turned green.

Salem sat up suddenly, his nose twitching. "I like cheese."

"Your envy is showing, Aunt Hilda." Sabrina helped herself to one of the cheese snacks.

"Is it?" Hilda pointed up a dish of fancy chocolates and popped one in her mouth. "These should neutralize the jealousy effect."

"I like chocolate, too," Salem hinted broadly.

"Chocolate isn't good for cats." Sabrina nodded approval as Hilda's skin tones returned to normal. "Much better, Aunt Hilda. Pea-soup green is *not* your color."

Forcing a smile, Hilda turned back to Vesta. "So—what else should we know about . . . what's-his-name?"

"Ashton. Ashton Whittier."

"Ashton Whittier," Salem drawled. "That has an old-money, country-club ring to it." His ears perked forward with sudden interest. "Blue blood and blue-chip stocks?"

"No." Vesta shook her head.

"New money, then?" Zelda asked.

"I don't know." Vesta shrugged. "How much does a university history professor make?"

Zelda sat back. "Not enough to support *your* lifestyle, Vesta."

"Not enough to support *our* lifestyle!" Hilda added.

"I'll adjust," Vesta said, dismissing their concern with a casual wave.

"That might not be so easy." Sabrina didn't want to burst Aunt Vesta's blissful bubble, but her Other Realm aunt didn't have a clue about the cost of mortal living. Or the hassles, either!

"You can't use magic as freely in the mortal world as you do in the Other Realm, Vesta." Zelda leaned forward intently. "There are a lot of restrictions."

"Oh, I know! But I've been keeping track of all your activities here for a long time." Smiling brightly, Vesta shifted her gaze between her two sisters. "Trust me. I won't make the same mistakes."

"Was that an insult?" Hilda glanced at Zelda and ate another chocolate.

"I'm not sure." Zelda poured herself another cup of tea.

Sensing the mounting tension, Sabrina decided a

diplomatic diversion was required. "I didn't know professors came in gorgeous, dashing, and charming. I always pictured them as stuffy old windbags."

Vesta laughed. "Believe me, Ashton is *not* a stuffy old anything!"

"Don't tell me." Hilda's forced smile tightened into a pained, thin line. "He's brilliant and has a great sense of humor, too."

"Yes!" Vesta grinned.

Zelda smiled with genuine affection and clasped Vesta's hand. "I'm really happy for you, Vesta. If there's anything we can do to help—"

"Well, now that you mention it—" Vesta stood up and took a deep breath, then glanced back when Salem tapped her on the shoulder.

"Would you mind picking up that can of tuna by your foot?" the crafty cat asked. "I dropped it on my way to the can opener."

Vesta picked up the can and dropped it on the counter, then graced her sisters and Sabrina with a pleading look. "I need your help planning the wedding, and I want to have it here."

"Here." Hilda eyed Vesta suspiciously. "In Westbridge?"

"Yes! In your wonderfully quaint, mortal home!" Vesta spread her arms. "It's *perfect* for a small ceremony—"

Hilda and Zelda looked at each other aghast.

"—next Saturday."

Hilda snapped her head around to stare at Vesta. "A week from today?"

22

"That's not much time to plan a wedding," Zelda said.

Enchanted by the idea, Sabrina enthusiastically threw her support behind Aunt Vesta. "We're witches! We can *point* everything we need for a wedding. What's the problem?"

"Would someone mind opening this?" Salem nudged the tuna can up to the can opener with his nose. However, he couldn't lift it up to the magnetic blade mechanism.

Vesta flinched. "Actually, there is one little problem. I want a *mortal* wedding, and I'm not inviting anyone else from our side of the family."

"Vesta!" Zelda's eyes widened. "That's *two* pretty big problems!"

"That's the understatement of the century." Hilda jumped to her feet and glared at her older sister. "Do you have any idea what an eccentric family of snubbed witches will do to us?"

Salem leered at them over the rim of the unopened tuna can. "If I'm lucky, they'll turn you all into fat mice and put me in charge of dispensing the cheese!"

Sabrina shuddered. Considering that most of the Spellman relatives she had met during the past year barely met the minimum standards for sanity, the family's potential for vengeance was not pleasant to contemplate. Then again, their retaliation for being left out might be less risky than having them all gathered in the living room at the same time. Either way, the potential for domestic disaster was huge.

"Why would you want to exclude the rest of the family, Vesta?" Zelda asked.

Vesta rolled her eyes, as though the answer to that should be obvious. "Because I haven't *told* Ash I come from a family of crazy witches."

"Why not?" Hilda pressed.

Vesta hesitated, then flinched when the doorbell rang, breaking the uncomfortable silence. "Uh-oh."

" 'Uh-oh?' I'm afraid to ask." Zelda covered her eyes.

Vesta smiled sheepishly. "Did I forget to mention that I invited Ash over to meet you?"

"That's him? At the door? Now?" Hilda glanced down at her dirty sweats, then paled when Vesta nodded.

"So Ash doesn't know we're all bonkers?" Sabrina asked pointedly. "Or he doesn't know we're all witches?"

"Both!" Vesta shrugged apologetically. "I, uh—just haven't gotten around to telling him—yet."

Make that domestic Armageddon!

"All right. There's no need to panic." Zelda held up her hands, taking charge and remaining calm. "We've had a lot of practice acting like regular mortals around Sabrina's friends."

"I wouldn't ask *them* for any references," Sabrina said. Harvey and Val had had more than one harrowing experience with magic gone awry in the Spellman household, not the least of which was being terrorized by the sadistic Molly Dolly Cousin Beulah had sent to entertain them last Halloween.

24

The doorbell rang again and Vesta swept out of the kitchen to answer it.

"Okay." Zelda zapped herself into clean slacks and a short-sleeved blouse. "We can keep this situation under control, if we just take things one step at a time."

"First step." Hilda pointed, exchanging her dirty sweats for a skirt and matching knit pullover.

Sabrina opted for jeans, a sleek tank top, and a more positive outlook. "Well, at least the house is clean!"

The dryer buzzer buzzed. The trash compactor door banged open and closed, and the dishwasher began flinging clean dishes around the kitchen.

"Break's over!" Salem cringed as a plate sailed over his head and smashed on the floor.

Hilda caught a coffee cup, then ducked to avoid a barrage of ballistic silverware. "Can we panic now?"

"Yes!" Zelda squealed as the carpet shampooer raced in and ejected a container of dirty water at her feet.

"Yes!" Salem shouted as the can opener magnet drew the tuna tin off the counter and clamped on. The blade bit into the tin and cut the top off. The cat jumped off the counter to peer into the lower cabinet. "Now, let's see what else we've got in here. Yum! Pretty Kitty Seafood Treat. One of my favorites!"

Sabrina didn't have time to argue when Aunt
Zelda delegated her to handle mortal damage control. She raced through the house to the foyer and
braked abruptly. It wasn't hard to figure out what
had happened in the past couple of minutes. Aunt
Vesta had opened the front door to let Ashton in
just before the appliances had gone back to work.
When Vesta had opened the hall closet to hang up
Ashton's tweed jacket, her unsuspecting mortal
fiancé had been ambushed.

Six feet tall and fortyish with a thick mop of
sandy-blond hair, Ashton Whittier was a hunk
plus, in spite of the jacket, button-down shirt, and
jeans that marked him as an academic. He was
definitely an academic with a renegade streak.
Under normal circumstances, he was probably
poised and confident. Being cornered by a single-

minded shoeshine machine determined to polish his leather loafers was hardly normal, and Sabrina didn't blame him for shaking in his shoes, wide-eyed and speechless with shock.

"Stop! Go away!" Hovering behind the aggressive shoe shiner, Aunt Vesta waved the jacket to chase it off, which had absolutely no effect. As far as Sabrina knew, this was the first time her vivacious aunt had ever been in a situation where she *didn't* want to confound or torment a mortal with magical mischief. Ashton didn't know that Vesta was a witch, and Vesta had *no* experience using her powers so a mortal wouldn't notice.

"Heel!" Sabrina pointed from the hip, latching on to the shoeshine machine with an invisible mini-tractor beam and hauling it away from Ashton's feet.

"Thank you, Sabrina!" Dropping the jacket, Vesta grabbed Ashton's hand and gazed into his warm brown eyes. "Are you all right?"

"Uh, fine." Ashton nodded, clearing his throat. "I think."

"Sorry about that, Mr. Whittier." Sabrina picked up the shoeshine machine and tucked it under her arm. She extended her other hand. "I'm Sabrina."

"Hello, Sabrina. Call me Ash, please." Ash smiled tightly and gestured at the machine. "What is that? Some kind of new, high-tech security sentry?"

Aunt Vesta eyed her niece narrowly.

"No! It's a—" Sabrina faltered, struggling to

come up with a feasible explanation. "It's, uh—an experimental model of a computer-programmed shoe-shining machine. It's, uh, incredibly dedicated. Guess the manufacturer hasn't worked all the bugs out yet."

"It's infested with insects?" Vesta grimaced. "Why do you keep it in the house?"

Ash laughed. "You have such a marvelous sense of humor, Vesta!"

"I do?" Bewildered, Vesta yanked Ashton out of the way when the vacuum cleaner zoomed by with the mini-vac cavorting behind it like a playful puppy.

Sabrina quickly rose to the challenge of explaining the inexplicable. "My aunt Hilda and aunt Zelda are suckers for every new gadget that comes out. They bought the whole line of, uh, Robotic Household Helpers."

"Indeed?" Ash linked his arm through Vesta's, his face beaming with adoration. "Where are your sisters?"

Vesta shot Sabrina an anxious look. "Where are they?"

"In the kitchen. The dishwasher threw a tantrum. They'll be out as soon as it calms down." Sabrina laughed nervously. "I'm going to take Shoe-bot here upstairs and give him some scuffed boots to polish and buff. Why don't you two wait in the living room?"

"Is it safe?" Vesta tightened her grip on Ash's arm and snuggled against him.

"It is unless you're a cat!" Yowling, Salem scrambled around the corner and bounded up the stairs. The automatic cat groomer rolled to a halt at the base of the stairs, then used its pincer claw arm to pull itself up one step at a time.

"Did I just hear that cat talk?" Ash asked.

"No!" Vesta shook her head in vigorous denial.

"Of course not!" Sabrina exclaimed. "The machine is programmed to act and talk like *it's* a cat. Personally, I don't think it'll ever get the Good Cat-Grooming seal of approval." Desperate, Sabrina shouted for reinforcements. "Aunt Hilda! Aunt Zelda!"

"Coming!" Aunt Hilda walked into the foyer with an inane grin on her face and a handheld mixer with spinning beaters in her hand. "Hello. You must be Ashton. I'm Hilda."

"How do you do?" Ash smiled graciously and pointed at the mixer. "Is that another Robotic Household Helper?"

Hilda blinked. "A what?"

"Yes, it is!" Sabrina chimed in. "Aunt Hilda just loves to cook, especially since she got the Mix-and-mash-bot."

"Right." Hilda's plastic smile remained fixed. "But if it doesn't shut off *soon,* I'm going to feed it to the Slice-and-dice-bot."

The beaters stopped.

"They're also interactive," Sabrina said.

Aunt Vesta glared at Hilda, as though she was

deliberately trying to sabotage Ashton's introduction to the family.

Ashton, however, seemed impressed. "That is simply amazing!"

"Isn't it?" Hilda shoved the mixer into Sabrina's free hand as Vesta pulled Ash into the living room. "Take this upstairs and give it a sink full of lotion to mix or something."

"Okay. I've got to rescue Salem from that groomer thingie anyway, but I didn't want to leave Aunt Vesta alone with all these machines going berserk." Sabrina lowered her voice. "We didn't tell her about the injunction against using magic for housework, remember? She doesn't *know* we're in the middle of an appliance rebellion."

"She is a little flustered, isn't she?" Hilda's satisfied grin segued into a frown. "Serves her right for snaring Mr. Absolutely Perfect. I can't even get a Mr. Totally Wrong to return a phone call or a toaster note!"

Spotting the sickly green hue of jealously spreading across Hilda's cheeks, Sabrina zapped up a handful of chocolates and gave them to her. "Ash seems really nice, and he adores Aunt Vesta. Don't do anything to spoil it, okay?"

"All right." Slumping, Hilda chewed one of the chocolates. "She'd just make me pay for it, and I don't want to go through the rest of my life wondering if every man I meet is really a plaster garden gnome."

A horrible feline screech resounded through the

upstairs hall, followed by thumps, hisses, yowls, and mechanical clanks and whirs.

Leaving Hilda to cope with the downstairs situation, Sabrina ran up the stairs. The cacophony of noise stopped abruptly when she reached the landing.

"Salem?" Sabrina glanced through her open bedroom door. Except for the digital alarm clock, which was flashing its hour and minute numerals with blinding speed, nothing in the room moved. "Salem! Where are you?"

The cat didn't answer, but the bathroom door flew open and the cat groomer rolled out waving jointed arms with brush, comb, scissors, and hair clip attachments. An electric shaver, the travel hair dryer, a lighted vanity mirror, and a curling iron formed a conga line behind it. Spotting Sabrina, the cat groomer paused as though it was sizing her up.

Sabrina raised a warning finger. "Take one more step toward me and you're scrap metal."

Startled, the groomer rolled back, then whirled and fled into Aunt Zelda's room with its entourage. Sabrina set the shoeshine machine down just inside the door and steered it toward the closet. Aunt Zelda had dozens of shoes and boots that would keep it occupied for several hours. The cat groomer and its beauty salon associates were already clustered in front of a glass display case, eyeing a sixteenth-century powdered wig. Unlike Hilda, who hoarded everything she had ever owned in the dungeon, Zelda was a discerning collector. Although she maintained that no one looked good in a powdered wig, this one had once belonged to a French aristocrat and had historical as well as sentimental value. When the cat groomer extended its pincer arm to unlatch the cabinet, Sabrina zapped a padlock onto the clasp and conjured up a pile of discount store wigs. Then she left to look for Salem.

The mixer beaters spun in anticipation as Sabrina went into the bathroom and opened the medicine cabinet. A muffled sob came from behind the shower curtain as she poured hand lotion, cuticle remover, makeup base, and cold cream into the sink. The mixer righted itself and set about whipping the basin of goo as Sabrina stepped toward the tub. "Salem?"

"Nooo!" the cat wailed. "Don't look."

"Come on. It can't be that bad." Sabrina drew the curtain aside and gawked, trying not to laugh.

Salem cowered in the corner. Every hair on his sleek body had been curled into a kinky corkscrew, and a huge, blue bow adorned his tail.

"Okay," Sabrina said. "It's bad, but it could be worse."

"How?" Salem looked up, sniffling pitifully.

"Well, the bow could be pink."

"And that's suppose to make me feel better?" Hanging his head, Salem sighed. "I'll never be able to show myself in the alleys of Westbridge again."

"You shed, Salem. It'll fall out eventually."

"Until then, I'm confining myself to quarters." Jumping out of the tub, Salem slunk to the door and scanned the hall. He bolted into Sabrina's room and slammed the door.

Sabrina decided against trying to coax him out. His growling stomach would overrule his wounded vanity within the hour, and she really didn't want to explain his instant perm to Ashton.

Back in the living room, Sabrina perched on the arm of the couch. Aunt Zelda had joined Hilda, Vesta, and Ash, and no appliances were in evidence. Judging from the industrious hum of whirring motors coming from the kitchen, Zelda had convinced or bribed them to stay out of sight. Sabrina helped herself to a cracker from the tray on the coffee table and dunked it into a bowl of salmon-colored dip.

"Welcome back, Sabrina." Ash raised a cup of tea in salute. "We were just about to discuss the guest list."

"Can Harvey and Val come?" Sabrina bit the dip-coated end off the cracker. "Great dip, Aunt Zelda. What is it?"

Zelda shrugged. "Just something the blender whipped up from the various cans the can opener had already opened."

Sabrina almost choked and dropped the rest of the cracker on the floor. Salem had been using the can opener, and she wasn't particularly fond of Pretty Kitty Seafood Treat, regardless of how good it tasted. She looked down as the mini-vac zipped out from under the sofa, sucked up the cracker, then ducked back into hiding. No one else seemed to notice.

"Immediate family only from our side," Vesta said.

Zelda made a notation on a pad.

Ash kissed Vesta's hand, making her blush. "Who's going to give you away?"

"No one!" Vesta's eyes flashed with indignation, and the room brightened with a flash of lightning. "I'm a totally independent wit—uh, woman!"

Ash recoiled, crushed by Vesta's anger and startled by the boom of thunder. "I know, Vesta. I just meant—"

"I'm sure my dad would love to walk you down the aisle, Aunt Vesta," Sabrina said quickly. Aunt Vesta was even more clueless about mortal ways than she had realized. The potential for disaster seemed to be increasing with each passing minute. "That's the best part of the *ceremony!* Except for kissing at the end."

"Oh! Of course!" Vesta forced a laugh, then cooed at Ashton. "Just teasing, dear. I'm sorry."

"You're forgiven, my love." Relieved, Ashton puckered up for a quick kiss, which Vesta didn't hesitate to give him.

Hilda wrinkled her nose in jealous disgust and munched another chocolate as a precaution.

"Edward and I haven't seen much of each other in the past century. Uh, I mean, year!" Vesta cleared her throat to cover the slip. "It just *feels* like a century. Maybe he won't want to do it."

"Yes, he will," Zelda said. "I'll leave a message on Ted's page to call me—"

"Pager," Sabrina said, correcting Zelda's reference to her father's page in *The Discovery of Magic*, the magic book her aunts gave her for her sixteenth birthday. "It's a pager."

"Right." Wincing slightly, Zelda continued. "He might want to bring Gail, too."

"Maybe. Maybe not," Sabrina said. "A wedding might get her seriously thinking about marriage again."

Sabrina only saw her father outside the pages of her magic book one weekend a month. He was a warlock with a busy life of his own in the Other Realm, which included the beautiful golden brown witch lawyer Gail Kipling. Although he loved her, he wasn't anxious to settle down again just yet. However, Sabrina realized, she would have to make sure he brushed with a tooth duller so he wouldn't *ping*. The definitive sparkle that flashed from her Dad's brilliantly white teeth was enchanting, but impossible to explain to mortals.

"I suppose one of you"—Vesta gestured at Zelda and Hilda—"should be the Old Maid of honor."

Hilda bristled. "That's *maid* of honor and Zelda would be delighted, I'm sure."

"No . . ." Zelda spoke with exaggerated, phony sweetness. "I don't mind if *you* do it, Hilda."

Sabrina had known her aunts long enough to recognize the beginnings of another major domestic disaster if she didn't stop it *now*. Neither one wanted the maid of honor distinction, but they didn't want to hurt Aunt Vesta's feelings, either. "Why don't you decide later?"

"Or *both* of you could do it!" Vesta's eyes shone with happiness as she eased a little closer to Ash. "That's a good idea, isn't it, darling?"

"Anything less is entirely unacceptable," Ashton said. "Beauty and charm obviously runs in your family."

Hilda nudged Zelda. "Maybe we could clone him."

Zelda didn't dignify the remark with a response. "But if we're *both* in the wedding party, no one but Ted and Sabrina will be sitting on the bride's side of the room."

"Harvey and Val would love to come and sit on Aunt Vesta's side," Sabrina hinted broadly. The wedding and reception wouldn't be nearly as much fun without her friends around to take the edge off the adult atmosphere.

"I don't have any family, but there are a few people from the university I'd like to invite," Ash said. "The head of the history department and his wife, Bernard and Sadie Morley. And Stephen and Crystal Hancock and my research assistant, Marla Thompson."

"Don't you have any attractive, single *male*

friends?" Hilda picked up the teapot to refill her cup.

"Actually, yes, I do. An old college buddy of mine lives in town. Will's single and I'm going to ask him to be my best man."

Zelda eyed Ash expectantly, her pen poised over the pad. "Will?"

"Willard Kraft, the vice principal at Westbridge High."

No fun! Sabrina stared at Ash. Mr. Kraft was the ultimate party pooper! However, that annoying fact faded into insignificance as chaos threatened to expose their mortal charade.

Chapter 5

Stunned by Ash's announcement, Hilda dropped the teapot on the edge of the snack tray. The other end of the tray flipped up, catapulting crackers onto the floor and overturning the bowl of dip. "Sorry!"

"I'll get it." Vesta instinctively raised her finger to point away the mess.

"No!" Sabrina grabbed Vesta's wrist, stopping her before she blew her mortal cover. "That's why we have Robotic Household Helpers."

The mini-vac rushed out from under the sofa, staking it's claim to the snack spill a few seconds before the vacuum cleaner and the carpet shampooer arrived from the kitchen. The three appliances circled the mess, motors racing like dogs snarling over a bone.

Curious, Ash reached down to pick up the mini-vac.

"Don't—*hic*—touch it!" Zelda covered her mouth, and the phone popped off the library table. Ash pulled his hand back.

"It bites!" Sabrina winced as the phone reappeared on the piano. Aunt Zelda had inhaled sharply at the mention of Mr. Kraft's name, which had resulted in hiccups and a short-circuit in her magical control.

"Excuse me—*hic!*" Zelda sprang to her feet.

The flower arrangement on the piano popped to the coffee table.

"Try a teaspoon of lemon juice," Ash suggested. His cup vanished a second after he set it down. Fortunately, his gaze was fastened on Zelda as she bolted from the room. "Was it something I said?"

"Don't be silly! Zelda's just, uh—" Vesta cast a helpless look at Hilda, then grabbed Ash's hand and dragged him toward the door.

"Weddings always unnerve Zelda," Hilda said. "Niagara Falls will become Niagara Drip before she becomes the bride again."

"I heard that!" Zelda yelled from the kitchen. *"Hic!"*

Hilda's chair popped out from underneath her, dumping her on the floor. "Did you do that on purpose, Zelda?"

Sabrina dropped her face in her hand. Having Mr. Kraft dropped into the wedding equation had tripled the disaster potential. Mr. Kraft had latched on to Aunt Zelda after Aunt Hilda dumped him. Sabrina didn't know if Aunt Hilda really liked the stodgy vice principal and regretted her decision, or if she just resented his interest in her sister. To keep peace in the family, they didn't discuss it much. However, if Mr. Kraft was going to be Ash's best man, the awkward situation would have to be addressed.

"Nice meeting you all!" Ash waved.

"Later!" Sabrina waved back, then sagged as Aunt Vesta shoved him out the front door and slammed it.

"Is he—*hic*—gone?" Zelda walked back into the foyer holding a slice of lemon. The potted ivy on the cabinet by the French doors popped out. She put the lemon slice in her mouth and grimaced.

Vesta collapsed against the front door and nodded numbly.

"Okay, Vesta!" Hilda brushed herself off and stomped into the foyer. "We've got to talk."

"Right." Sabrina caught the ivy when it reappeared in thin air and set it back on the cabinet. "You've got to tell Ash you're a witch before we all have nervous breakdowns."

"Absolutely. Pretending to be a mortal takes years of practice." Zelda paused and cocked her head. "What do you know? The lemon cured my hiccups!"

"Turnip root and dried snake skin boiled in daisy nectar tastes better," Hilda said.

"But it takes two weeks to ferment and only works half the time." Zelda tossed the lemon peel into the living room, where it was immediately surrounded by the mini-vac, vacuum cleaner, and shampooer.

Sabrina saw Salem creeping down the stairs. As she had expected, hunger and the aroma of dumped fish dip were more compelling than preserving his dignity. He tried to slink behind Hilda and Zelda without being seen, which was sheer feline folly. Sometimes she was certain her aunts really did have eyes in the back of their heads.

"Nice perm, Salem." Hilda glanced over her shoulder. "But ditch the bow."

"It's glued on!" Sobbing, Salem scampered into the living room. "Oh, no! The vacuum cleaner beat me to the dip!"

Sabrina felt genuinely sorry for the cat, but she was more worried about Aunt Vesta, who was always calm, confident, and in control. Nothing in the Other Realm or mortal world ever fazed her! However, *acting* like a mortal for an hour had turned her into a pale, shaken, borderline basket case. If she didn't tell Ash she was a witch soon, Aunt Vesta would be a blithering idiot before she said "I do."

"You look like you need to sit down, Aunt Vesta."

"Yes," Zelda said. "You're obviously suffering from magic withdrawal."

"What I *really* need right now is some fresh air!" Vesta flicked her finger with a flourish.

Sabrina screamed, scared and thrilled when she suddenly found herself shooting white-water rapids

41

in a raft with her three aunts. Vesta had, appropriately, pointed them all into wet suits and life vests for the wild ride. Water sprayed over the bow as the rubber boat bobbled around rocks and dipped into swells. Steep canyon walls whipped by as the swift current carried them downriver.

Clinging to a safety rope, Zelda shouted to be heard over the thundering rapids. "Vesta! I can't hear myself think and we have to talk!"

"In a minute!" Manning the tiller oar, Vesta struggled to keep the raft on course and upright.

"How come that roaring noise is getting louder?" Sabrina yelled.

Hilda's eyes widened as she pointed forward. "Because we're headed for that waterfall up there!"

"What waterfall? I don't see—" Sabrina screamed again as the raft suddenly plummeted over the edge of a hundred-foot drop. "We're all gonna—"

"—have something wickedly gooey to eat," Aunt Vesta said calmly.

Sabrina, Hilda, and Zelda abruptly stopped shrieking when they realized everyone in the quaint sidewalk cafe was staring at them. Vesta had exchanged their white-water attire for casual, but chic, slacks and blouses and had dried and styled their hair. Sabrina would have preferred jeans and a tee but was too relieved and enthralled with her surroundings to complain. The Eiffel Tower pierced a clear blue sky in the background and the startled waiter sputtered indignantly in French.

"Mesdames! S'il vous plaît, dominez!"

"What did he say?" Sabrina leaned forward, whispering.

Zelda shifted uncomfortably. "He's just politely pointing out that we've betrayed ourselves as crass Americans."

"I can deal with that." Sitting back, Sabrina sighed. "We're alive and I feel great!"

Hilda nodded. "Near-death experiences have that effect."

The waiter impatiently tapped his order pad with his pencil. *"Qu'est-ce-que vous desirez?"*

"Quatre fudge-brûlant glaces avec crème-fouettee et les noix." Vesta's smile was radiant, her cheeks still flushed with excitement.

"I can't eat a hot-fudge sundae with whipped cream and nuts!" Hilda gasped, appalled. "I might as well get a direct infusion of fat!"

The waiter bowed slightly and left mumbling with disgust. *"Americains."*

Vesta's radiant glow dimmed as she patted Hilda's hand. "Yes, you can. You'll need it."

"Why?" Sabrina loved hot fudge, but Aunt Vesta's sudden change in demeanor was troubling. "Does it have anything to do with potential domestic disaster?"

"Correct me if I'm wrong," Zelda said, "but haven't we been coping with domestic disaster all day?"

"Yes." Hilda leveled Vesta with an accusatory glare. "Most of which could have been avoided if

Vesta had told her mortal fiancé that he's marrying into a family of witches *before* she invited him over to meet us."

Vesta smiled tightly. "Yes, well—there's the problem. I'm not going to tell him. Ever."

"What?" Sabrina, Zelda, and Hilda exclaimed in unison.

"Why not?" Zelda added.

"Yeah!" Hilda exhaled with exasperation.

"Because," Vesta explained with unruffled calm, "if I had to choose between turning Ashton into rocks or losing my magic, I'd choose magic. That's why."

Vesta's reasoning was sound, Sabrina realized. If a witch confided her magical nature to a mortal and that mortal betrayed her, there were only two options. Within twenty-four hours, the witch had to turn the mortal into a pile of rocks or forfeit her magical powers.

"It's not that I think Ashton would deliberately betray me," Vesta went on, "but things can go wrong. Sophia's fiancé was tricked into betraying her secret."

Sabrina nodded soberly. Sophia was a Spellman ancestor who had chosen to relinquish her magic rather than sacrifice her true love. Centuries had passed before Sabrina had stumbled onto the problem in Rome and helped right the wrong that had been done.

Hilda's mouth fell open. "Drell will declare amnesty for all would-be world conquerors before you'll be able to keep your witch identity a secret from Ash, Vesta. You almost blew it half a dozen times just this afternoon!"

"I know." Vesta frowned, then brightened. "That's why I came to you! So you can show me how to cover myself!"

Zelda laughed, then coughed self-consciously when the waiter returned with their sundaes. When he left, she pushed her sundae aside. "It won't work, Vesta. We've been living in the mortal realm for a long time, and *we* can't get along without using magic on an everyday basis."

"And we've got a house full of underworked appliances to prove it!" Sabrina took a bite of her sundae. "That hits the spot."

Hilda nibbled her lip, her gaze shifting away from the sundae and back again until she finally succumbed to the temptation. "I have *no* willpower. Oh, well." Picking up her spoon, Hilda attacked the dessert with reckless abandon.

"But I really do love Ash and I have to try." Vesta looked at them imploringly. "Will you help me?"

"I will," Sabrina said emphatically. "Love is a great motivator, and I think Aunt Vesta can do anything she sets her mind to."

"All right." Zelda slumped in surrender, then pointed a warning finger at Vesta. "But I want your word of honor as a witch that you won't cheat by using magic."

Vesta raised her hand. "I swear on my witch's honor."

"Great!" Sabrina raised a spoon dripping with vanilla ice cream and hot fudge. "So much for potentially disastrous domestic consequences for all!"

"I'll eat to that!" Hilda grinned.

Vesta averted her gaze and toyed with her parfait.

"Is there something else you haven't told us, Vesta?" Zelda asked.

"Well—" Vesta put her spoon down and folded her hands on the table. "I suppose we will have to do something about the Spellman spinster curse."

Chapter 6

Sabrina shut off the all-purpose garage vac and hauled the cumbersome machine over to the kitchen sink. They had popped home from Paris to discover that the dishwasher had smashed another load of clean dishes before running through another wash cycle with its door open. Sabrina was mopping up the flood while Vesta swept up broken dishes and Hilda dried the walls. Aunt Zelda was feeding a cranky garbage disposal while she waited for the dishwasher to finish a load of pots and pans. The mess in the kitchen was inconvenient, but the damage wasn't permanent and it certainly wasn't as potentially cataclysmic as the Spellman spinster curse!

"Excuse me, Aunt Zelda. I have to dump the dirty water." Sabrina dropped the end of the hose in the sink as her aunt moved aside.

"With pleasure. I'm running out of things to stuff

47

down the disposal's gullet anyway. The refrigerator is almost empty." Wiping her brow with her forearm, Zelda despondently sank onto a chair.

Wearing a ruffled apron, Vesta held the dustpan at arm's length and dumped another batch of dish fragments into the trash compactor. The door slammed closed, trapping the edge of the plastic dustpan. "Hey! Let go!"

"A word of advice, Aunt Vesta. Let the machine win." Sabrina pointed the garage vac off the floor so the water could flow downward through the hose. "And stick with mortal world appliances after you're married. They don't always work right, but they don't need major attitude adjustments."

Vesta let go of the dustpan and jumped back as the trash compactor swallowed it whole. "There must be a better way to keep a house clean without using magic! Somehow, I can't picture Oprah spending quality time with a broom."

"She doesn't have to." Hilda climbed down off the stepladder and tossed a wad of soggy paper towels toward the compactor. "She can hire someone to clean."

"Hire someone?" Vesta ripped off her apron and sat down. "If I can *pay* someone, why am I learning how to do all this?"

"Because you can't afford a housekeeper on a history professor's salary." Zelda turned in her chair and opened the cabinet under the sink counter to get more cans for the can opener. "What are you doing in there, Salem?"

"Hiding!" Salem cautiously stuck his head out. "Do you have any idea what it's like to be trapped in a house where appliance anarchy reigns?"

"It can't be any worse than finding out you're doomed to lose the love of your life and die an old maid!" Sabrina lowered the empty garage vac and joined her aunts at the table.

"You mean, it's true!" Hilda whined. "I had almost convinced myself I'd wake up and find out this was all a horrible nightmare."

"No such luck," Sabrina grumbled.

Aunt Vesta stiffened under Sabrina, Zelda, and Hilda's annoyed scrutiny. "Would you all feel better if I hadn't told you? At least, now you know *why* none of the Spellman women ever find lasting love and happiness."

"You mean there's a reason?" Salem jumped onto the counter. "Beyond the who-could-spend-more-than-a-century-with-the-same-witch-anyway factor?"

Depressed, Sabrina dropped her chin on her folded arms. None of them had been prepared to deal with Aunt Vesta's shocking story or confession.

"I just want to be sure I understand all the facts." Aunt Zelda remained admirably calm as she recounted the significant details. "Our great-grandfather, Cornelius, jilted Gertrude to marry our great-grandmother, Daphne."

"Right." Vesta nodded. "And since she was the witch scorned, Gertrude exercised her vengeance rights and cast a spinster spell over Daphne's white wedding shawl."

"Which turned the shawl black during Cornelius and Daphne's marriage ceremony a thousand years ago," Zelda continued.

"And hasn't been seen since because a huge falcon stole the shawl right off Daphne's shoulders and flew off with it." Hilda glowered at Vesta.

"And without the shawl Gertrude's spinster spell can't be broken," Zelda finished. "Which explains why Cousin Marigold's marriage to Harold ended in divorce and Drell left Hilda standing at the altar."

Hilda's eyes narrowed. "And why Zelda's marriage to music-man only lasted three days!"

"And why Roland has a perpetual crush on *me!*" Sabrina gasped.

"The spinster spell was probably a contributing factor," Vesta said.

"And here I thought being romantically challenged was a Spellman family trait," Salem quipped.

"Apparently, it is. It's just not genetic." Hilda frowned suddenly. "How come Zelda and I didn't know about this family curse before, Vesta?"

"Because I'm the oldest. Mother passed the secret and the responsibility of trying to solve the problem on to me." Vesta shrugged nonchalantly. "Until I found Ash, I never had a good reason to worry about it."

"That is so like you, Vesta!" Hilda's temper flared to the boom of thunder. "I don't suppose it ever occurred to you that Zelda and I might have lost the loves of our lives because of this, did it?"

"Actually, no." Vesta cocked her head. "Did you?"

"How would I know?" Hilda wailed. A small, dark misery-cloud appeared over her head. "I only attract arrogant weirdos like Drell and stuffed-shirt losers like Willard Kraft!"

"Willard's very sweet, Hilda." Zelda paused thoughtfully. "I *was* rather fond of Galileo—until he didn't credit me for my contributions to his theory of constant acceleration due to gravity."

"But all of that is *so* ancient history!" Sabrina looked up desperately. "I'm worried about current events. Like Harvey!"

"And Ashton," Vesta said. "So we have no choice except to find the spinster shawl and break the spell."

"I won't argue with that." Calming down, Hilda waved the misery-cloud away. "Do you have any idea where the shawl is?"

Vesta shook her head. "No."

"Gertrude has it stashed somewhere, no doubt." Rising, Zelda began to pace. "I might be able to establish her last known location through the Witches With a Grudge directory. And there's a remote chance I can get a lead on the shawl with a Missing Cursed Objects computer search."

"Maybe you could curse that stupid cat groomer and tell it to get lost," Salem muttered.

"Assuming I find the shawl," Zelda continued, "how difficult is the reversal spell, Vesta?"

"I don't know."

Sabrina groaned, which attracted the drifting misery-cloud. "You don't have a clue? Nothing?"

"Not specifically," Vesta said. "All I know is that

a Spellman bride has to wear the shawl at her wedding."

"There's got to be more to breaking the spell than that." Hilda stood up abruptly. "Everyone is on research detail until further notice."

"I'll check with the Keeper of the Index in my magic book," Sabrina said. "He has *everything* cross-referenced—"

"Incoming!" Hilda squealed and ducked. "Frying pan at twelve o'clock!"

Vesta deflected the flying skillet with a quick point.

Sabrina hit the deck and threw her arms over her head as the dishwasher discharged the rest of the clean pots and pans. After the last lid clanged against the wall, she slowly got to her feet.

"Well, that could have been worse." Zelda picked up a dented saucepan. "They didn't break."

"Wish I could say the same for my heart," Sabrina sobbed. After everything they'd been through, including her temporary infatuation with Dashiel, she could still lose Harvey because of some stupid, ancient spite spell. Nothing could be worse than that!

The misery-cloud hanging over Sabrina's head suddenly unleashed a downpour, drenching her and flooding the kitchen again.

Chapter 7

☆

☆

Sabrina sat cross-legged on her bed with the phone cradled in her lap. "Come on, Harvey! Answer!"

"Please!" Curled up on the end of the bed, Salem groaned. "I've spent more exciting Sunday afternoons watching shadows creep across the floor."

"You have reached this number," the answering machine message said for the hundredth time. "You know who you are. We don't! Heh, heh, heh. No one is available to take—"

"No one has been available at Harvey's house since Friday night!" Sabrina slammed the receiver down and flopped backward. "How come Harvey isn't home watching sports on TV?"

"Maybe he is," Salem said. "Or maybe *he* had a family emergency. Or maybe the ringer on his

53

phone is broken. Or maybe he's tried to call you and *our* call waiting isn't working. Or maybe—"

"All right, all right. I get the point." Sabrina set the phone aside. There probably was a perfectly logical reason why she hadn't heard from Harvey. She just hoped it wasn't because the spinster spell had kicked in and Harvey wanted to bail out of their relationship.

Blat. Blat. Blaaaat. A misery barometer popped into the room with klaxon blaring. The mood indicator needle dipped to minus-nine below "devastated."

"Storm watch!" Salem yelled and sprang toward her with his tail tucked underneath him.

"Oops!" Sabrina zapped an open umbrella into her hand as Salem slipped under her arm. They both cringed as the hovering misery-cloud released another drenching rain. She drew her knees up, pulling her feet out of the puddle pooling in the middle of her bed.

"I can't take many more of these close calls, Sabrina. Cats are allergic to water applied externally."

"I know. Have cloud, will shower." Sabrina sighed. "But how can I get un-miserable when being miserable gets me rained on and makes me *more* miserable?"

"Look on the bright side," the cat suggested. "The carpet shampooer and the garage vac are getting in so many work hours cleaning up after your misery storms, they'll qualify for the Mars luxury overhaul by Wednesday!"

"Great!" Sabrina stared through the sheets of rain streaming off the umbrella. The misery-cloud had enlarged in direct proportion to her deepening depression. Everything within a four-foot radius was being drenched. "Then *I'll* have to clean up after my cloud!"

"Why not just get rid of the cloud?" Salem asked solemnly.

"I wish." According to Aunt Zelda, misery-clouds weren't conjured. They were a *para*-paranormal phenomenon specific to witches, a physical manifestation of the metaphor *dampened spirits*. They just appeared, and getting rid of them wasn't easy. The requirements varied with each individual.

"As I recall," Salem said, "Hilda just waved it away."

"Yeah, but it didn't leave. It attached to me." Sabrina moved closer to the wall to escape the encroaching puddle. "Why? I mean, Aunt Hilda didn't suddenly get happy. She was still upset about the missing shawl and the spinster spell."

"True, but the misery-attraction was broken when she decided to research the problem to solve it." Salem nodded sagely. "The power of positive thinking was an Other Realm concept first, you know."

"No, I didn't know, but maybe you're right!"

Sabrina brightened. She had been sulking in her room since they had finished cleaning last night. Not being able to reach Harvey had pushed her deeper into despair, which had just strengthened the bond with the dark cloud. "So maybe if I *do* something positive, like go see the Index Keeper, Walker comma something-or-other, the cloud will go away."

The torrential downpour subsided to a drizzle.

"Hey! It's working! Sort of. Thanks for the tip, Salem."

"You're welcome. Now if you'll excuse me, I have to find a dry spot to finish my nap." Salem jumped over Sabrina's lap and sprang toward the door, forgetting to tuck his tail, which had been curled into a corkscrew spiral.

"I see the Groomer thingie cornered you again."

"Don't rub it in! Zelda's electric curlers and the electric toothbrush joined the Feline Beauty Gang. Now *I* ping!" Salem curled his lip back and a bright sparkle flashed off his left fang.

Sabrina laughed, then laughed harder when the drizzle stopped. The misery-cloud was still there when she closed the umbrella, but she didn't let that curb her rising spirits. As long as she kept an upbeat, positive attitude, maybe she wouldn't have to go to school tomorrow with the annoying cloud hanging over her head.

"The fearless flood brigade is here." Salem stepped aside to let the carpet shampooer and the garage vac enter. He paused to make sure the hall was clear of beauty bandits, then darted out.

Relieved that the appliances were eager to mop up so she didn't have to, Sabrina transformed into a stream of glittering golden sparkles and dived into her magic book. Her magical molecules reassembled in the hall outside the Index Office, and she quickly suppressed her dismay when she realized the misery-cloud had traveled with her.

Putting on a happy face, Sabrina entered the antiquated office. Nothing had changed since she had used the index to find Gail to apologize for damaging the lawyer's relationship with her father. The old wood furnishings included two card catalogs, a stool, two desks, and assorted bookshelves, all of which were piled high with books and files. A lighted candle and a stuffed Rolodex sat on each desk. Curled charts hung on the walls, and two parakeets sat on perches in a hanging cage by the far wall.

"Hello!" Sabrina glanced at the transparent transport tube on the left. The short, thin Index Keeper whooshed down and stepped out. As usual, he was dressed like a turn-of-the-last-century clerk in a white shirt with sleeve garters, a brown vest, brown pants, brown bow tie, and a brown visor. His abrupt manner hadn't changed since her last visit, either.

"Walker comma James T. at your service." The efficient little man peered at her intently through thick glasses.

"Spellman comma Sabrina J. We've met before."

The Index Keeper started. "Didn't you find what you were looking for?"

"Yes, I did. Thanks. Kipling comma Gail on page eight seventy-five. I'm looking for something else this time."

"I don't have a 'something else' category," Walker comma James T. said sternly. "You'll have to be more specific."

"Right. I'm looking for a white wedding shawl—"

"Getting married, huh?" The Index Keeper cocked his head. "That explains the misery hyphen cloud over your head."

"No, it's not for me. It's for my aunt."

"Women's Apparel, Bridal Department. Pages nine-sixteen through nine thirty-four. Good day!" Bowing curtly, the Index Keeper picked up a box of loose Rolodex cards and sat down at the large desk.

"No, I don't want to buy one. I want to find one that's been missing for the past thousand years."

Walker comma James T. didn't look up as he pulled the Rolodex toward him and began inserting cards. "Lost and Found. Page three forty-three. However, they're not responsible for items left unclaimed for more than five centuries."

Frustrated, Sabrina counted to ten to calm herself. She didn't want her reference privileges revoked because her misery hyphen cloud had rained in the Index. "It wasn't lost. It was stolen."

"Stolen!" The Index Keeper looked up sharply.

"Police Department. Theft comma petty. Page five twenty-two."

"Is that my only option?" Although she wasn't guilty of anything this time, Sabrina's previous encounters with the Other Realm cops had not been exactly pleasant, and she prudently tried to avoid them. For all she knew, there were laws against having misery-clouds that weren't housebroken.

"All criminal references are forwarded to the OR Police files."

Sabrina blinked, wondering why he was sending her to Oregon. Then she realized OR was short for Other Realm.

"The tube will take you. Don't forget to bend your knees." The Index Keeper sighed as he returned to his filing. "Now where in the blazes comma blue was I?"

Sabrina entered the transparent transport cylinder, punched the desired page on a keypad, and closed her eyes. The tube whisked her directly to her destination. Her stomach lagged a few seconds behind.

Like the Index Office, OR Police Precinct #13 looked like a set in a 1940s black-and-white movie. A smoky haze hung over a room full of old desks, manual typewriters, rotary dial phones, coffee cups, and doughnuts. Everyone was talking; uniformed officers, detectives with rolled up shirtsleeves and brimmed hats pushed back off their brows, stylish female reporters looking for a scoop and various perps—mostly trolls, Sabrina noted with interest as she stepped out of the tube.

A short man with a paunch and the shadow of a beard paused on his way by. "What's a nifty dame like you doing in a place like this?"

"Uh—looking for theft comma petty?"

"An index referral, huh?" The man jerked his thumb over his shoulder. "Detective Kolwalski. Third door on the left." He looked back as he moved off. "And make sure that misery-cloud of yours doesn't have any accidents in here."

"No problem! I'm happy!" Sabrina flashed him a dazzling smile, then scowled up at the cloud. "Watch it or I'll have you evaporated in the nearest tanning salon."

The cloud darkened and dripped.

Sabrina shook the water droplets off her nose and knocked on Detective Kolwalski's door.

"Yeah, it's open!" a gruff voice barked. A young man whipped his feet off a cluttered desk and swiveled his chair around as Sabrina stepped inside. Detective Kolwalski diplomatically ignored the misery-cloud hanging over her head and motioned her to have a seat. "What seems to be the problem, Miss—"

"Spellman comma—I mean, Sabrina Spellman." Sabrina sank into the lumpy, leather chair and sighed. "I have to find a shawl that was stolen from my family by a witch named Gertrude a thousand years ago."

"A shawl?" Scowling, the detective pointed to a metal filing cabinet, opened the third drawer down, and flipped through the files.

Sabrina's hopes rose as a folder rose out of the drawer and zipped into his hand. If Gertrude had a rap sheet, maybe the police knew where to find her. "What's that?"

"The Spellman comma Sabrina J. file." Leaning back, the detective thumbed through the papers in the folder. His frown deepened when he tossed the file on his desk.

"What?" Sabrina asked anxiously.

"Seems like you've been in trouble with OR Law before." Kolwalski arched a questioning eyebrow.

"When?" Sabrina shifted uncomfortably under his hard gaze. She *had* been pulled over for an emissions violation on her way to a Magic Pumpkins concert once. She hadn't known that flying a vacuum with a full bag and trailing dust was an environmental infraction. "Okay, but I was let go with a warning for dust pollution! And I've been keeping my vacuum tuned up and the dirt bag empty ever since!"

"I was referring to your attempt to take over the mortal world," Kolwalski said. "That's an offense punishable by a hundred years in cat confinement."

"Yeah, I know, but that wasn't my fault," Sabrina huffed defensively. The OR cops had busted her in her own bedroom right before she had launched her first assault against Westbridge High. If Salem hadn't figured out why she had been acting like

61

Libby and visa-versa, she'd still have ninety-nine years to go as a feline familiar. "My personality got switched with the local megalomaniac's because of sunspot molecular instability. We lost half our furniture to a black hole in the kitchen sink."

Kolwalski nodded. "That particular storm kept the department jumping for days."

"So what about my family's shawl?"

"Sorry, but no report was filed at the time of the crime." Kolwalski shrugged. "The statute of limitations expired three hundred years ago."

"But I don't want Gertrude arrested and charged with stealing it. I just want to get the shawl back! It's a matter of life and love!" The misery-cloud rumbled, reacting to Sabrina's sudden surge of desperation. "Please."

The detective rubbed his chin, then zapped up a form and a pencil. "Okay. Give me a description and the details, and I'll see what I can do."

"Great!" Sabrina took a deep breath and blurted out the story again. The detective stopped her cold.

"Wait, wait!" Kolwalski dropped his pencil. "Are you saying that Gertrude put a revenge spell on the shawl before she stole it?"

"Right. It turned black before the falcon flew off with it." Sabrina glanced at him warily. "Is that a problem?"

"It is for you. Gertrude exercised her vengeance rights and the shawl was legally cursed, so it's not a police matter."

"But there must be something you can do!" Sabrina pleaded.

"I can't, but you might try a Missing Cursed Objects computer search," Kolwalski suggested.

Exactly what Aunt Zelda was trying to do. With no leads to follow, Sabrina thanked the detective and took the transport tube to the nearest book exit. She rematerialized by her bed to find that the appliances had finished cleaning up the water. However, Aunt Vesta was pulling handfuls of dirt out of a bag and flinging the dirt around the whole room.

"Aunt Vesta! What are you doing?"

"Oh, there you are, Sabrina!" Vesta flashed her a smile. "Zelda asked me to help so I'm dusting your room."

Sabrina ran her finger over the top of her dresser, drawing a line in a quarter-inch layer of fine powder. "Didn't Aunt Zelda explain what dusting meant?"

"No. I looked it up." Pointing, Vesta conjured a hologram of the definition according to *Webster's Dictionary.*

> *vt.* 1: to sprinkle with dust or a fine, powdery substance.

"Thanks." Sabrina didn't have the heart to explain that the third definition, 'to rid of dust by wiping or brushing away,' was the pertinent one.

"There! All done." Shaking the residue off her hand, Vesta waved as she headed out the door. "Now I'm going to scour the bathtub. Although, I'm not sure what I'm supposed to be looking for."

"That's scour as in 'clean by rubbing vigorously,' Aunt Vesta!" Sabrina called after her. "Not 'search thoroughly'!"

Vesta stuck her head back in. "Whatever. As soon as I'm done, Hilda wants you to take me grocery shopping. The garbage disposal will be finished with the grass clippings soon, and she doesn't want to sacrifice the roses."

"Sure." Sabrina perched on the edge of the bed and lifted her feet to let the mini-vac clean underneath them. Grocery shopping with Aunt Vesta was the perfect way to end a totally dismal day.

She hadn't heard from Harvey, and their relationship was still ultimately doomed because she had run into a complete dead end trying to find the Spellman spinster shawl.

Now her room had been turned into a mini-Sahara and she had been delegated to brave the local supermarket with a witch who thought "produce by the pound" meant choreographing tap dancers in an OR stage musical.

The cloud rained, turning the dust on Sabrina's bed into mud.

Chapter 8

☆

☆

Sabrina absently listened to Val complain as she stashed her afternoon books in her locker and loaded up for her morning classes.

"—one of the most *boring* weekends of my life!" Val sagged against the wall. "Not that my social life *ever* rises to the level of gossip worthy news. No offense."

"None taken," Sabrina said lightly. Things were looking up to a degree and she didn't need anything remotely resembling a bad mood, even by association.

She had laughed herself to sleep last night after shopping with Aunt Vesta, an experience that had been more amusing than annoying. Determined to be a good mortal wife—a joke in and of itself, Sabrina thought wryly—Aunt Vesta had spent fifteen minutes trying to find the most perfect peach in the bin. Then she had carefully read the ingredients and vitamin percentages on every box of cereal and fretted over the fat content versus the price per pound of ground beef. They would have been in the store all night if Sabrina hadn't reminded her that the garbage disposal wasn't picky about the menu. After that, Aunt Vesta had taken mischievous delight in finding the most gross and least costly foods the market had to offer and devising sickening recipes they had dubbed "garbage gourmet." Consequently, Sabrina had awakened in a good mood under a clear, misery-cloudless ceiling.

Val slammed her locker closed. "Grounding me for coming home a little past curfew Friday night was totally out of line, wasn't it? It's not like we were out pushing over cows or drag racing down Main Street or anything." Val paused, frowning. "Sometimes I think my mom and dad take their parental responsibilities *way* too seriously."

"I can't argue with that." Sabrina grinned. There were definitive advantages to having witches for guardians. Mortal parents weren't distracted from meting out deserved punishment by rampaging household appliances or side trips to Paris for dessert. On the other hand, mortal teens didn't have to coach precocious aunts in the art of living magic-free or track down cursed family heirlooms that posed a serious threat to their happily-ever-after romantic aspirations.

Depression alert! Sabrina shook off the negative

thoughts and glanced upward. The air above her was still clear, but there was no guarantee the misery-cloud wouldn't return if sufficiently provoked.

"I mean," Val went on, "technically speaking, I could say I was chaperoning you and Harvey. Wait. I *did* say that. They didn't buy it."

Harvey! Sabrina suppressed a flutter of anxiety. Just because no one at the Kinkle house had answered the phone all weekend didn't mean he was mad at her or that something terrible had happened.

"They wouldn't even let me use the phone, which is why I didn't call." Val cocked her head. "Did you call me?"

"Well, no. Things got a little hectic around my house." Sabrina scanned the hallway, looking for Harvey. He almost always stopped by her locker on his way to first period. So where was he today?

"How come?" Val fell into step beside her as they headed down the hall.

"Would you believe I went white-water rafting and ate a hot-fudge sundae in Paris?" Sabrina asked flippantly, trying to keep a lid on her mounting concern.

"No." Val laughed, then looked at Sabrina askance. "Did you?"

"Actually, I spent most of the weekend doing housework," Sabrina said honestly, evading a direct answer to the question. "And my other aunt is visiting this week. She's getting married and wants to have the ceremony at *our* house next Saturday."

"A wedding?" Val shifted from depressed basement doldrums to enthusiastic flying high, her boring weekend instantly forgotten. "I love weddings!"

"Who's getting married?" Harvey asked as he came up behind them.

Sabrina did an abrupt about-face. "Hi, Harvey. How's it going?"

"Well—" Harvey shrugged with a resigned grin and scratched his neck. "My uncle called Saturday morning and invited the whole family up to the lake. Then my dad and I spent the whole weekend scraping the bottom of his boat. I guess I had an okay time—except for the mosquitoes."

"Cool!" Sabrina beamed, silently chiding herself for worrying about nothing. "Not that I'm glad you're covered with bug bites. I just, uh—wish you had called me to let me know you'd be gone. So I wouldn't worry." She quickly added, "About whether or not something had happened to you."

"We left too early to call, and my uncle's cabin doesn't have a phone." Harvey scratched another spot behind his ear. "Did you call me?"

"A couple of times." Sabrina's eyes narrowed warily. "Why?"

"There must have been a hundred hang-up calls on our answering machine." Harvey exhaled shortly. "I hate that."

"Me, too." Sabrina smiled tightly and glanced at

Val, who was peering at the pink blotches of calamine lotion dotting Harvey's arms.

"You know," Val said, "I think if you connect the pink spots it spells 'Yo!'"

"The bugs were a picnic compared to being ambushed by my little brother and cousins." Harvey leaned closer to the two girls and whispered. "They painted my toenails red while I was sleeping. I didn't even notice until I took my shoes and socks off to help launch the boat last night."

"Well, that's better than noticing in the locker room showers after practice," Sabrina offered brightly.

"I suppose, but they're still red." Harvey shook his head. "I tried sandpaper, but it just took the skin off the tips of my toes."

Sabrina put her hand behind her back and pointed up a small bottle of nail polish remover. "Here. Try this."

"Hey! Thanks. My mom was out of this stuff." Harvey nodded, smiling. "It's amazing how you always have just what I need when I need it."

"I've noticed that." Val turned back to Sabrina. "So can I help with the wedding?"

"Now that you mention it—" Val's ability to change subjects with no warning never ceased to amaze Sabrina. This time her timing was perfect. "My aunt Hilda is handling the details, but I'm sure she'll appreciate any help she can get. And the whole thing will be more fun for me if you two are involved."

"I don't know anything about weddings," Harvey said. "I suppose I could tie tin cans to their car bumper or something."

"You can be the usher, Harvey," Sabrina suggested enthusiastically. "You'll look great in a tux."

"Those little bow ties snap on, right?" Harvey asked.

Sabrina dashed toward first period math marveling at how most of her problems and the misery-cloud had disappeared overnight. Finding the spinster shawl was Aunt Zelda's sole priority, and Sabrina was confident she would succeed. Aunt Hilda had grudgingly agreed to make all the wedding arrangements, and although she was basically clueless, Aunt Vesta was taking her mortal lessons seriously. Harvey wasn't mad at her—and in retrospect she realized it had been foolish to worry—and now she had good reason to invite him and Val to the wedding. As a bonus, the week had started *without* a before-class, verbal duel with Libby.

Not bad for a Monday.

"How much? For a few bunch of flowers? I'll get back to you." Incredulous, Hilda slammed down the phone and stalked into the kitchen. When she had been forced to take charge of the wedding plans, she had had no idea how complicated a simple ceremony could be. Or how costly—in hard-earned mortal dollars! Something Vesta had no concept of whatsoever. A crash course in mortal economics was imperative.

The phone rang once, then stopped as Hilda paused in the kitchen doorway. Curiosity prevented her from interrupting the confrontation between the dishwasher and Vesta, who had volunteered to take over the household chores.

"Oh, no, you don't!" With a broken plate in one hand and a cracked cup in the other, Vesta held the dishwasher door closed with her foot. More broken china was strewn across the floor.

Vesta looked gorgeous even though her auburn curls were tangled and she was wearing borrowed sweats, Hilda noted, annoyed. She was also fighting mad.

"You may have an injunction against the use of magic in this house, but if you don't stop throwing dishes all over the place, there won't be anything left to wash! Then how will you meet your work requirement?"

Curled up on the counter by the can opener and surrounded by empty cat-food tins, Salem opened one eye when the dishwasher began to shake.

Vesta raised her finger. "I can't use this to do your work, but I *can* use it to shut off your power source and water supply!"

The can opener raised its blade in alarm. The cat quickly calmed his new best buddy. "Don't worry. She's bluffing."

"No, I'm not!" Vesta's eyes flashed a warning as she whipped her unruly hair behind her ear and turned her finger on the trash compactor, which banged its door open and closed, demanding a handout. The garbage disposal spit out a mutilated plastic bottle cap coated with shredded garbage.

Hilda crossed her arms and leaned against the doorjamb. It wasn't often she had the satisfaction of seeing Vesta on the verge of losing it. In fact, she had *never* seen Vesta so flustered before.

"Quiet!" Vesta tossed the broken cup and plate into the compactor, then reached for the empty cat-food cans on the counter.

"Wait!" Salem sat up, appalled as the tins disappeared into the appliance. "I didn't lick that one clean, yet!"

"What's going on here?" Zelda stopped beside Hilda.

"Vesta's taming the kitchen wildlife. Who was on the phone?"

"Willard," Zelda said casually. "He wanted to make sure Vesta would be here when Ash comes over later. Something about the wedding, but he wouldn't tell me what."

Hilda stiffened with irritation but didn't pursue the matter. Willard had become fair game after she had stopped dating him, and she didn't want to admit, even to herself, that maybe she had made a mistake. It wasn't like Zelda was madly in love with the annoying old coot or anything, but—her heart flip-flopped—that might change *after* they found the spinster shawl and removed the spell!

"Attention!" Vesta zapped the overhead light. The bulb sputtered, popped, and went dark.

The unruly appliances stopped shaking and

banging, and Hilda's wandering thoughts snapped back to the kitchen. Vesta squared her shoulders and adopted a stance that reminded her of Sergeant Slater at Witch Camp.

"You will all start behaving properly *now* or the power goes *off,*" Vesta barked. "Do I make myself clear?"

Silence.

"Why didn't we think of that?" Zelda whispered to Hilda.

Hilda shrugged. "Maybe we've just gotten too comfortable with constant chaos."

"That's better," Vesta continued. "You will all calculate how many work hours you need to accumulate by midnight Friday. I'll work out a schedule that ensures everyone will meet the requirements for luxury overhauls. Anyone who throws dishes or tantrums, creates floods, instigates food fights, or disobeys a direct order will be penalized. You *will* have hours deducted. Agreed?"

The machines whirred in somber ascent.

Hilda and Zelda applauded.

"I'll be in charge of the can opener," Salem purred. "However, I refuse to volunteer for cat-groomer duty on the grounds that it *is* harmful to my feline sense of dignity."

"I'll see what I can do, Salem." Vesta glanced at her sisters with a triumphant smile, but her tone bore an infuriating trace of smugness. "So—are you two making any progress?"

"No." Zelda pouted. "Legitimate vengeance

spells and related cursed objects from a thousand years ago are protected by Ancient Codes."

"Since when can't you hack through a security code?" Hilda asked, surprised. "Especially one that's obsolete."

"Not computer codes," Zelda clarified. *"Codes.* Like in code of honor, code of chivalry. All the old rules and regulations are intact even though the information has been entered into the OR mainframe."

"That's why Mother was never able to find the shawl." Vesta sighed.

"I may have to make an appointment with the Witches' Council to get a dispensation." Zelda picked up a broken plate. "Just to remove the file security ward so I can locate the spinster shawl. We'll have to remove the curse ourselves."

"What makes you think Drell will give *us* an exemption?" Hilda moved aside when the mini-vac crept out of hiding to clean up the small glass splinters.

"Are you kidding, Hilda?" Vesta laughed. "Drell's life will be so much less troublesome if you find someone else and settle down for a while. He'd never admit it, but he still feels guilty about not showing up for your wedding. Tea anyone?"

Zelda nodded.

"With a pinch of milkweed antacid powder," Hilda specified. "Thinking about Drell always gives me heartburn."

"Thinking about you makes Drell break out in

purple hives." Vesta started to point, then caught herself. She filled the kettle and turned on the stove by hand. "I do believe I'm getting the hang of this!"

"Bravo! Why don't you practice pouring the cat a bowl of milk," Salem suggested.

"What did you find out about the flowers, Hilda?" Vesta opened the dishwasher and pulled out two mugs and a teacup—the only unbroken mugs and teacup left in the house.

"They're expensive. Using magic would be much more cost effective and efficient. For one thing, there's no extra charges tacked on because of the short notice."

"No." Vesta shook her head. "If I can adjust to living without magic, you can arrange a little wedding."

"You just killed a lightbulb with your finger!" Hilda protested.

"Only to make a point," Vesta argued.

"How many shops did you call?" Zelda dropped the broken plate in the trash can. The compactor started to protest, then thought better of it and quietly closed its door.

"One." Hilda frowned uncertainly.

"No, no, no. You've got to comparison shop, call around to get the best price." Zelda glanced at the clock. "And I've got to contact the Witches' Council scheduling desk."

"Call around?" Hilda complained as she followed Zelda back into the living room. "But I've still got to find a justice of the peace and arrange for the cake and the invitations and decorations. Even with speed dial I'll wear out my pointing finger!"

Vesta held the milk carton over Salem's bowl. "Is it my imagination or is everyone more stressed than usual?"

"Around here it's hard to tell." Salem sighed. "Pour!"

☆

Chapter 9

☆

"Hey, Gordie!" Sabrina waved.

The surprised science whiz froze in the hallway outside Mr. Kraft's office. "Are you talking to me?"

"Yeah. Don't wait for me to start the Science Club meetings this week. My aunt's getting married and I won't be able to make it."

"Okay. Thanks." Gordie smiled awkwardly. "I hope she's happier than we were."

"So do I." Sabrina sighed as Gordie continued on his way. She and Gordie had been paired in a trial marriage for a class assignment. It had been a disaster, not through any fault of his, but because she had spent the whole week ignoring him and worrying about Harvey's partnership with Libby. The cheerleader had taken advantage of the situation to win his heart for real. Harvey hadn't fallen for Libby's conniving efforts, but Sabrina had almost spoiled her relationship with him because of her mistrust. In the end they had patched things up, and Mr. Kraft had given her and Gordie an A for realism. She sincerely hoped that Aunt Vesta and Ash flunked realism and enjoyed a wonderful life together.

Provided they actually *had* a wedding on Saturday, which seemed a lot less likely since Sabrina had talked to Aunt Hilda during lunch. Frazzled and frustrated, Aunt Hilda had begged her to bring Val home after school to lend a hand. *Not literally,* Sabrina thought with a bemused grin. Being a witch, it was necessary to qualify figures of speech that mortals used with reckless abandon. "Cat got your tongue" had a decidedly different connotation in the Other Realm. Aunt Hilda had also assured her that the appliances wouldn't be running amok. Val was unbelievably dense sometimes, but even she wouldn't be able to ignore a swarm of flying hair dryers or dueling vacuum cleaners.

And she better not leave Val waiting at the front entrance too long, either. Val's insecurities didn't need an excuse to run wild, and Sabrina didn't want to spend fifteen minutes explaining that she wasn't having second thoughts about letting her help with the wedding.

Sabrina turned to head back down the hallway just as Libby stormed around the corner.

"Out of my way, freak!" The cheerleader sneered

as she brushed by. *"I* have an important meeting with Mr. Kraft."

"And this is supposed to annoy me?"

Libby didn't bother to respond, but Sabrina did a double take as the girl barged into the school office. The vice principal's door was open, and Ashton Whittier was seated in front of Mr. Kraft's desk. Libby marched in without waiting to be invited and closed the door.

What could Mr. Kraft, Libby, and Aunt Vesta's fiancé possibly have in common?

Nothing.

Except—the wedding?

An uneasiness just shy of near-panic seized her.

"Wish I was a fly on the wall so I could hear what's going on." Too much of a stretch, Sabrina realized. Even magic had its limits. However, something a bit larger and just as easily concealed might work!

Sabrina ducked into the nearest rest room, stashed her books in a stall, and zapped the grate over the ventilation into temporary oblivion. "Okay. Here goes."

> *"Tiny does as tiny be,*
> *make a monkey out of me."*

Sabrina pointed and gritted her teeth. Her ears popped as the spell engaged, instantaneously changing her into a small, grayish-brown spider monkey. She caught a glimpse of her reflection in the mirror as she scrambled onto the sink.

Cute—for a scrawny furry thing with a bald face, a ski-jump nose, glittering black eyes, and no lips.

As makeovers went, Sabrina thought she had looked better as a cat. However, her long monkey arms and prehensile tail were ideal for climbing into and quietly navigating through the ventilation ducts. Guided by the sound of Libby singing, Sabrina quickly reached the vent that opened high in the wall of Mr. Kraft's office.

"Listen, do you want to know a secret—"

Sitting back on her hairy haunches, Sabrina peered through the grate. Libby sat in a chair beside Ash, but she wasn't actually singing. She was guardedly watching Mr. Kraft and Ash as they listened intently to a cassette recording. Aunt Zelda was fond of the Beatles, a British rock and roll group that had dominated the world music scene in the 1960s and '70s, and Sabrina recognized most of the songs in the medley. The scene looked suspiciously like an audition, an ominous indicator that was temporarily dismissed when she caught the scent of fresh fruit. Her alert simian eyes quickly located the shiny, red apple sitting on Mr. Kraft's desk.

"—will you still feed me when I'm sixty-four?" Libby's demo tape ended with a dynamic guitar chord progression.

"Was I right or what?" Mr. Kraft hit the Off

button on the small tape recorder. "Isn't she fabulous?"

"You were right, Willard." Ash grinned at Libby and nodded his approval. "She's great!"

Addicted to attention and praise, Libby accepted the compliment with her usual lack of graciousness. "Yes, I am, aren't I?"

Sabrina listened absently, her gaze riveted on the apple. She wanted it. More than anything.

"Willard thought you might be interested in singing at my wedding this Saturday, Libby," Ash said. "Now that I've heard you, I'll be thoroughly disappointed if you refuse."

Libby sing? At Aunt Vesta's wedding? Sabrina was appalled by the thought, but more overwhelmed by her monkey priorities and senses. She wanted that apple!

"How much does it pay?" Libby asked.

"The vice principal will be grateful. *Very* grateful." Mr. Kraft ejected the cassette tape and slipped it into a plastic case.

Libby shrugged. "That sounds like an offer I can't refuse."

Sabrina pushed on the grate, then ducked back when the noise drew Mr. Kraft's attention.

"Did you here that?" Mr. Kraft asked.

"I didn't hear anything," Libby said.

"I'll have to check with my fiancée first, of course, but I'm sure she'll agree, Libby." Rising, Ash took the cassette tape from Mr. Kraft's hand.

"I'll go play this for her right now and let you know this evening, Willard."

Sabrina tensed as Ash left the office, her thoughts on the Libby problem, her gaze still fastened on the apple. If she got home before Ash arrived, she might be able to convince Aunt Vesta that having Libby sing at the wedding was a really bad idea. Ash wouldn't press the issue if his beloved objected.

But if she went home now, she'd have to forget about the apple, which wouldn't be a dilemma for Sabrina the teenage witch or Sabrina the teenage girl. Sabrina the spider monkey didn't even consider it. She hunkered down to wait until Mr. Kraft and Libby left.

"Thanks, Libby. I knew I could count on you. Ash was my best friend in college. My only friend, actually."

"That's okay, Mr. Kraft." Libby lanced him with a barbed smile as she stood up to leave. "Just don't forget it the next time *I* need a favor."

"Of course not." Mr. Kraft nervously adjusted his glasses and cleared his throat. "Uh, there *is* one other thing you should know about the wedding. Mr. Whittier is marrying Vesta Spellman, Sabrina's aunt. At Sabrina's house."

"Really?" Libby paused to calculate how she could use that to her advantage. Her deliberations lasted roughly three seconds. "Our cheerleader uniforms are starting to look a little shabby, don't you think? I mean, they weren't exactly hot five minutes ago."

"Uh-huh." Mr. Kraft jotted a note on a pad. "New cheerleader uniforms. Anything else?"

"I'm sure I'll think of something." Totally pleased with the bargain, Libby marched out the door victorious.

"I have no doubt." Mr. Kraft slumped, as though dealing with Libby had totally drained him of energy, which it probably had.

Sabrina curled her lip back in sympathetic disdain for the self-centered cheerleader, then scratched her hairy side. Her hungry gaze darted back to the apple by Mr. Kraft's elbow. She tensed in anticipation when he stretched, hoping he was finally going to leave. She totally lost control when he picked up the apple and took a huge bite.

Furious, Sabrina screeched and rattled the grate.

Startled, Mr. Kraft threw the apple over his shoulder and jumped to his feet. "What the— Who's there?"

Oops! Sabrina regained her wits as quickly as she had lost them. As Mr. Kraft picked up a ruler and cautiously approached the grate, she took off scrambling back through the duct, shrieking in alarm and frustration.

Returning to her normal form the instant she hit the rest room floor, Sabrina pointed the ventilation grate back into place, grabbed her books and ran out the door. The hall was deserted, and she darted around the corner just before Mr. Kraft charged out of the school office, screaming for the janitor.

Val was walking circles around a campus bench when Sabrina burst through the outside doors. "There you are! I thought maybe you had left without me."

"No, I just got delayed." Pouting, Sabrina headed down the sidewalk. "But I *didn't* get the apple!"

"It's about time!" Aunt Hilda's head snapped around when Sabrina and Val came in the front door. With her blond hair carelessly tied back and her eyes flashing wildly, she looked hopelessly panicked. "I've worn my fingers to the bone walking through the Yellow Pages!"

Val flinched, intimidated by Aunt Hilda's accusing tone. "I'll be right back."

As Val fled for the bathroom, Sabrina set her books on the piano and flopped into the armchair. There wasn't any room on the sofa. It was strewn with phone books and Aunt Hilda's disorganized notes.

"What took you so long?" Aunt Hilda asked petulantly.

"Sorry. The next time I decide to practice molecular transformation, remind me not to turn into a monkey." Sabrina pointed an apple out of thin air and bit into it as if she hadn't eaten in days.

"You won't need reminding," Aunt Hilda said. "For reasons nobody's ever been able to figure out, being a monkey has lingering aftereffects. I craved peanuts and chocolate-covered ants for a week."

"Ooh! Good idea!" Sabrina pointed again and a dish of normal-looking chocolates filled with crispy ants appeared on the coffee table.

"Is everything okay now?" Val hesitated in the foyer.

"Come on in, Val." Aunt Hilda cleared a corner of the sofa. "Maybe you can make some sense of this mess."

Sabrina stuffed three chocolates in her mouth.

Val perched on the edge of the sofa and surveyed the disarray. "Do you have a checklist?"

"No." Aunt Hilda shook her head. "Do I need one?"

"It would help." Val picked up the papers beside her and shuffled through them. "How about index cards and a card file?"

"That can be arranged. I'll be right back." Palming the apple core, Sabrina bolted for the dining room, where she zapped up two packages of three-by-five index cards, tabbed dividers, and a plastic file box. She dashed back into the living room and gave them to Val. "Here you go."

"Thanks." Taking a deep breath, Val opened the dividers and spread them on the coffee table. She ate one of Sabrina's ant-filled chocolates, then started to write. "We'll need a section for flowers, cake, invitations, guest list—"

"I'll be right back." Leaving Aunt Hilda in Val's capable hands, Sabrina dashed to the kitchen to get another apple. Halfway through the dining room, she heard the muted sound of Libby singing the Beatles song "And I Love Her" coming from the kitchen.

And suddenly remembered *why* she had been in such a hurry to get home!

Aunt Vesta and Ash didn't look up when Sabrina barged in. They were sitting at the table with a small tape recorder between them, listening to Libby's demo, holding hands and gazing inanely into each other's eyes.

". . . this love of mine will never die," Libby's voice sang. "And I love her. . . ."

Ash hit the stop button. "And I mean every word, Vesta."

"Oh, Ash—" Vesta blushed.

Oh, give me a break!

"I think having this girl sing at the wedding is a wonderful idea!" Vesta leaned forward to kiss Ash.

"No!" Sabrina grimaced when Aunt Vesta and Ash both turned to look at her. "I mean, uh— Libby and I aren't exactly friends."

"Then you can get to know each other better at the wedding." Vesta turned her big, brown eyes back on Ash, snagging his adoring gaze.

"But—"

Vesta clasped Ash's hand again. "Let's have her sing this medley of Bumblebee songs. They're perfect."

"Beatles," Ash corrected gently.

Sabrina didn't bother to argue. The happy couple had made their decision, and she didn't feel right saying anything that might tarnish their wedding. As it was, Vesta still had to worry about the spinster spell. Sabrina had to worry about the spell, too, and at last report Aunt Zelda hadn't made any progress finding the shawl.

Turning away, Sabrina zapped a handful of peanuts and succumbed to a moment of self-pity. Now, as though facing a life of unrequited love wasn't bad enough, she had to deal with the compulsive eating habits of a monkey and Libby's arrogant, obnoxious presence at the ceremony on Saturday!

Sabrina stiffened when she heard a low rumble. She looked up to see the misery-cloud hanging over her and quickly ducked into the laundry room before Ash noticed. Everything had gone downhill so fast so suddenly she didn't have the energy to rally and popped into her bedroom to brood. Val and Aunt Hilda would just have to carry on without her.

Salem peeked out from under her pillow and mewed anxiously. "Were you followed?"

"No. Why?"

Sighing, Salem flipped the pillow off his head, which had sprouted long, neatly braided dreadlocks. *"This* is why!"

"Compliments of the cat groomer, I assume. Do you know how much people are willing to *pay* for hair extensions?" Shoving the rest of the peanuts in her mouth, Sabrina zapped another apple and sat down on the bed.

"Ask me if I care!"

Sympathizing, Sabrina pointed up a bowl of Kitty Delight Shrimp Treats. "Here. Indulge yourself."

"Thanks. Vesta's got the can opener on a strict schedule and I'm starving."

Not exactly starving, Sabrina thought with a glance at the potbelly the cat had acquired since the can opener had started working overtime.

"So how was your day?" Salem stabbed a treat with a claw that had been painted neon green.

"Judging by appearances, about the same as yours. Miserable." Sabrina didn't even try to fight off her gloomy mood. She huddled under an umbrella with the cat, munching apples and nuts while it rained in her room.

Chapter 10

☆

After an hour of concentrated dejection, Sabrina decided to stop feeling sorry for herself so the cloud would go back to Misery Land or wherever it hung out when it wasn't hanging out over her. Lifting her bottomed-out spirits wouldn't be easy. Aside from the obvious reasons she had crashed into the basement of glum, she felt guilty about throwing Val into the witches' den without a safeguard—her. She hadn't felt or heard any major disturbances in the magical force that permeated the house, but then she had been totally immersed in self-pity, cut off from whatever had transpired beyond her circle of rain.

"Okay, Salem. We're getting out of here."

The cat peered over the edge of the bed. "There's six inches of water down there!"

"So?" Sabrina shrugged, unconcerned. She was

pretty sure the garage vac wasn't even close to having all its necessary work hours. Under ordinary circumstances, they never used it. Neither she nor her aunts had ever attracted a misery-cloud that routinely flooded the house before.

"I'm a cat! I'd rather face the groomer's Beauty Gang again than get my feet wet!"

"Your choice." Sabrina laughed and the misery shower stopped. "Hey! Cool. Come on. I'll carry you." She zapped away the umbrella and pointed on rubber boots.

"Directly to the can opener, please. Maybe we can sneak open a few cans when Vesta isn't looking."

"If Ash is still here, that won't be a problem. The roof could cave in and she wouldn't notice." Cradling the cat in her arms, Sabrina sloshed through the water into the dry hall at the top of the stairs and paused.

"Why did you stop?" Salem asked.

"We've still got company." Sabrina zapped off the boots.

Salem perked an ear to listen to the hushed murmur of conversation in the living room. "Val and Hilda are just addressing invitations."

"Not the problem." Sabrina rolled her eyes upward. The cloud wasn't dribbling water, but it was still there. "If it doesn't leave soon, I'll name it and then I'll *never* get rid of it."

"True, but since it's attached to you and not to me, I'll go it on my own from here." Salem squirmed until Sabrina set him down. He dashed down the stairs, muttering softly. "Let's see. Am I in the mood for caviar or smoked oysters?"

Shaking her head, Sabrina crept halfway down the stairs so she could hear without being seen from the living room. Of course, that's the moment Vesta chose to walk Ash to the front door. And naturally, Ash saw her before she could pop back upstairs. Smiling inanely, she waved at the hovering cloud, hoping it would rise out of sight.

"I'll see you soon, Sabrina." Ash waved back.

When he turned away to open the door, Sabrina caught Aunt Vesta's eye and pointed upward. Spotting the cloud, Vesta hustled Ash outside as thunder boomed through the house. Expecting another downpour, Sabrina sprinted up the stairs.

"Was that thunder?" Val asked.

"Probably just a car backfiring or something," Hilda said.

Sabrina paused on the landing as Aunt Zelda emerged from the linen closet wearing the tailored black suit she only wore to official Witches' Council functions.

"I got it!" Aunt Zelda waved a glittering paper, shaking off a shower of golden sparkles. Her grin faded when she saw Sabrina and her dark, soggy companion. "Still feeling depressed, I see."

"It's hard not to when fate seems determined to make my life miserable."

"We are masters of our own fate, Sabrina." Quick changing into jeans and a comfortable blouse, Aunt Zelda softened her stern expression. "What's the problem now?"

"Aunt Vesta and Ash want Libby to sing at the wedding."

"Oh." Aunt Zelda glanced at the misery-cloud and sighed. "Well, I suppose I could get used to having a leaky cloud around the house, but I'd rather not. Maybe this will help." She shook the sparkling paper again.

"What is it? A recipe for irrational-bliss blintzes?" Sabrina asked sullenly. "Jump for joy exercises?"

"No, it's a dispensation from Drell so I can bypass the ancient codes to locate the spinster shawl."

"Is that good?" Sabrina held her breath.

Zelda nodded. "Yes. Because now I've got a chance to find the shawl so we can break the spell."

"Way!" Sabrina didn't have to look to know the misery-cloud had vanished again. The surge of hope she felt was loaded with positive attitude.

"But Drell didn't grant the dispensation without exacting a price." Frowning, Zelda peered down the stairs as Vesta came back inside. She waved her to come up, then explained the bargain she had struck with the Head of the Witches' Council. "If we *don't* break the spinster spell by Saturday, Hilda will have to work a week as Drell's court jester *every* time she insults him."

"How incorrigible!" Vesta laughed softly. "Don't you just love Drell's twisted sense of humor?"

"No! That's a life sentence!" Sabrina's eyes widened with dismay. "Aunt Hilda can't even *think* about Drell without insulting him."

"I know, but I didn't have any choice." Zelda looked up suddenly, checking for the misery-cloud. When it didn't reappear over her head, she cheered up. "So I'll just have to find the shawl, won't I?"

"Yes!" Vesta nodded adamantly, her delight dimming. "Except we still don't know *how* to break Gertrude's spell."

"We'll figure it out, I'm sure," Zelda said confidently. "Don't worry. And do *not* tell Hilda about my deal with Drell. She'll make us all wish we had just let the curse stand."

"I won't," Sabrina promised as Zelda started down the stairs. "Ditch the pixie-dust paper, Aunt Zelda. Val's here helping Aunt Hilda organize the wedding."

As Zelda pointed the paper into her bedroom, the garage vac crept out of the bathroom.

"Halt!" Vesta ordered. "You're not scheduled to sweep the area for another hour."

The garage vac stopped, shaking on its wheels.

"Let it go, Aunt Vesta. My room's flooded again, and I hate having to wade to bed."

"You've got the most tenacious misery-cloud I've ever met, Sabrina." Shaking her head, Vesta waved the garage vac into Sabrina's room.

"She keeps feeding it!" Zelda threw up her hands. "What do you expect?"

When they entered the living room, Aunt Hilda

looked up from her address book with a worried, questioning frown. "How'd the meeting go, Zelda?"

"Mission accomplished." Zelda's vague, but positive response regarding the code dispensation was not lost on Hilda.

"Cool! Val and I are making great strides, too." Hilda glanced at Val quizzically. "Aren't we?"

"Absolutely. I've got to call about the cake tomorrow, but we got a terrific price on flowers. And these exquisite engraved invitations are ready to go." Pleased, Val tapped the small stack of sealed and addressed envelopes on the coffee table. "I'll mail them on my way home."

"Where'd you find a printer to deliver engraved invitations on such short notice?" Sabrina asked, then realized Hilda had zapped them, something Vesta had specifically asked her not to do.

"I'm very resourceful." Hilda shifted uncomfortably as Vesta wandered around the sofa and picked up the single unused invitation. The front was embossed with gold wedding bells. Inside, Ash and Vesta's names plus the time, date, and address of the wedding and reception were written in flowing gold script.

"This is lovely, Hilda." Vesta put the invitation back on the coffee table. "What's a bachelor party? Willard is throwing one for Ash Friday night."

"You're kidding, right?" Val hesitated when Vesta just looked at her blankly, then explained. "It's like a last fling for the guy who's getting married. Men only."

"Except for the singing telegrams—" Hilda clammed up suddenly. "Never mind."

Vesta's face darkened. "Doesn't the bride get a last fling, too?"

"Yes," Zelda said quickly. "But it's called a bridal shower."

"Ash gets a party and I get rain?" Vesta's peeved scowl deepened.

"No!" Sabrina laughed. "A shower *is* a party, but it's called a shower because—"

"Everyone you invite *showers* you with gifts!" Val grinned. "You should have one!"

"Excellent idea. I love opening presents." Vesta beamed. "Let's do that."

Zelda sank onto the arm of the sofa. "I suppose we could, but—"

"We'd have to get the invitations out today!" Val interrupted. "We don't have time!"

"That's not a problem." Vesta smiled knowingly at Hilda. "Is it?"

"No." Irritated, Hilda pointed to the high chest by the French doors. Val had her back turned and didn't see the small pile of cards and envelopes appear. "Funny how principle goes right out the window when parties and gifts are involved."

Ignoring Hilda's caustic sarcasm, Zelda suggested that they restrict the shower guest list to the women they had invited to the wedding. While Val and her aunts addressed the shower invitations, Sabrina excused herself to whip up a quick snack. First, she pointed up three bowls filled with apples, mixed nuts, and an assortment of honey-roasted insects. She ate something that looked disgustingly like a beetle.

"Even *I'm* not desperate enough to eat bugs." Perched on the counter, Salem covered his ears to block the crunching sound as Sabrina chewed. "Yuck!"

"I'm not thrilled, but they're actually not that bad. Try one." Sabrina offered the bowl.

"I'd rather not, thank you." Salem's dreadlocks flounced when he jumped to the floor.

"Where are you going?"

"To see if the cat groomer will consider a buzz cut. I'm getting a stiff neck from carrying these heavy braids around."

A tray of cheese, crackers, and sliced pears appeared with a flick of Sabrina's finger. Grabbing a fistful of nuts, she carried the tray into the living room just as Val was leaving to mail the invitations.

"Are you sure you want Libby at the shower?" Val pleaded with Vesta.

"It just *feels* like the right thing to do," Vesta said, looking a little bewildered.

Libby again! Sabrina stopped dead and fumbled the tray. Several crackers slid off onto the floor before Hilda righted the platter with a quick-draw point. Appliance motors started up in various corners of the house.

Sensing the impending vacuum invasion, Vesta gently shoved Val out the door. "You'd better get moving, dear. Thanks for all your help. We'll see you tomorrow."

"Bye, Sabri—" Val's shouted goodbye was cut off as Vesta slammed the door.

Whirling, Vesta confronted the floor-cleaning appliances rushing to the scene of Sabrina's cracker spill. "Ten-hut!"

The vacuum cleaner, mini-vac, and carpet shampooer scrambled into an orderly row and came to rigid attention.

"At ease." Hands clasped behind her, Vesta stared them down until they shut off their motors.

Sabrina watched in a daze. What cosmic clown had decided that Aunt Vesta couldn't get married without Libby Chessler? Mr. Kraft, she realized numbly.

"That is *so* annoying." Aunt Hilda glowered at Vesta and took the snack tray from Sabrina's hands. "Vesta always has to be better at everything than everyone else."

"Looks like she did her time at Witch Camp, too," Sabrina mumbled.

"Yes, but *she* was enrolled in W.O.T.C.," Hilda fumed. "Witches Officer Training Corps. Sergeant Slater loved her."

Sabrina couldn't even muster a chuckle. She had gotten used to dealing with Libby's condescending attitude and superior demeanor at school. Most of the time, she almost enjoyed the verbal parrying, but the harassment would totally spoil the wedding festivities.

"Would you mind going into the kitchen before your cloud soaks the carpet?" Aunt Hilda asked.

"The little drip is back?"

"Afraid so. And while you're at it, would you mail those wedding and shower invitations to the Other Realm?" Hilda nodded toward the coffee table. "Vesta decided to invite Gail to annoy your father. She's sending invites to our mother, too, even though there's no chance she'll come."

Sabrina grabbed the invitations and looked up sharply. "What if Grandma Spellman tells the rest of the relatives? Don't we have enough trouble without starting another family feud?"

"Mother's too embarrassed to tell *anyone* that her darling oldest daughter is marrying a mortal—" Hilda faltered with an apologetic grimace. "Sorry, Sabrina. I didn't mean that the way it sounded. Mother adores you even if you are—"

"Half mortal." Sabrina smiled. "I know."

"Good. Now, I think it's time to test the discipline in the ranks." Grinning impishly, Aunt Hilda tipped the snack tray, scattering cheese, crackers, and pear slices.

The carpet appliances started their engines and charged the mess, ignoring Vesta's attempts to organize an orderly cleanup.

Sabrina went back into the kitchen with her cloud, which was momentarily content just to rumble and not drizzle. Munching nuts and honey bugs with one hand, she dropped the invitations into the toaster with the other one by one. Aunt Hilda came rushing in as she sent the last envelope off.

"Did you pick up the extra wedding invitation that was on the table? I can't find it."

"I don't know, Aunt Hilda." Sabrina didn't react when Hilda absently scooped a few morsels from the bug bowl. "How many was I supposed to mail?"

"Four. Wedding and shower invitations for Gail and Mother." Hilda swallowed, then nodded approvingly. "These are good. What are they?"

"Honey-roasted grasshoppers, assorted beetles, and roaches. I mailed five."

"Five! Okay. Don't panic. The extra invitation wasn't addressed, so it'll just end up in the dead-letter file—" Hilda blinked, her mouth open in shock. "Did you say grasshoppers?"

The Other Realm Postmaster dropped the bundles of Witch-mart sale flyers he was stuffing into bulk-mail distribution tubes when the dead-letter bell rang. He frowned as a card popped up in the toaster that routed undeliverable mail from the mortal world to the main OR postal branch. Properly addressed letters were automatically sent to their final destination.

Sighing, the Postmaster pulled the card from the slot and turned to put it through the shredder for recycling. However, the gold embossed bells gave him pause. Curious, he opened the folded card. "What do you know? Vesta Spellman is getting hitched."

The Postmaster stared at the card, wondering what to do. It was common knowledge that Vesta spent very little time in the mortal world and probably had no idea how the inter-realm postal system worked. He did know one thing. *He* didn't want to be held responsible because no one showed up at her wedding!

Playing it safe, he dropped the card into the duplicating cauldron and programmed it to send invitations to *all* the members of the Spellman family.

Chapter 11

How do I look, Salem?" Sabrina studied her reflection in the antique, full-length mirror with a critical squint. The soft blue velour tee, black stretch pants, and black high-heeled boots looked great, but she thought it might be too casual for Aunt Vesta's bridal shower.

"Better than I do," Salem sobbed.

"This is true." Sabrina glanced back, feeling sorry for the cat. After the cat groomer had discovered buzz cuts, it had decided Salem needed a daily touch-up. Utilizing its unique concept of dramatic artistry, the ornery machine had left long tufts of fur at the tip of Salem's ears and tail, which made him look like a bald lion—with a paunch. *Not a pretty sight.*

"Will you bring me some of those shrimp canapés Vesta got from the deli?" Salem whined pathetically. "And some bacon crackers with liver paté? I can't go downstairs and beg for them myself looking like this. Strangers only feed cute cats."

"You look adorable, Salem"—Sabrina pulled her hair back with her hands, liked the effect, and pointed it into place with a large gold barrette— "for a black cat with a poodle-do."

"Go ahead. Rub it in. You can't possibly make me feel any worse." Salem sighed woefully, then looked up in sudden alarm. "Where's the little drip?"

"I got rid of him. Again."

"How'd you manage that?" Salem asked, genuinely curious. "It hasn't exactly been a carefree week around here. If stress had a market value, we'd all be rolling in dough."

"Tell me something I don't know. But to answer your question, I found out it's allergic to sitcoms."

Laughter induced by comedy had become Sabrina's quick remedy for chasing the misery-cloud away, but it wouldn't stay away. Every time she thought she was free of it, something happened to make her sad or mad, and the nasty little mist came back. Driven by desperation, she had finally resorted to research for help.

No one knew where misery-clouds came from or what attracted them to one miserable person rather than another. They were a rare phenomenon even in the OR. When they did mysteriously appear, they wouldn't disengage from the chosen subject unless they found someone more miserable in the immediate vicinity to attach to. Which is why *she* was plagued by it and not Aunt Hilda. The longer a cloud stayed, the stronger the bond became and the harder it was to shake loose. The only good news was that once the misery-cloud finally did attach to someone else, the previous bond was permanently broken.

On the other hand, her uncontrollable craving for monkey food had subsided on Thursday, two days after she had grossed out just about everyone she knew.

"Would you mind pointing up a sweater for me?" Salem's fuzz-covered skin rippled with a shiver. "I think I'm catching a chill."

Sabrina granted the cat's request, then waved away a hovering hair dryer and dodged the garage vac on her way to the dresser. Having ascertained that it rained more in Sabrina's room than anywhere else in the house, the bulky water vacuum had taken up residence when it wasn't patrolling the hall outside the bathroom. Sabrina chose a pair of long black earrings set with blue star sapphires from her jewelry box and slipped them on as she returned to her desk.

"Look out." Lying down, Salem drew his nearly naked legs under the warm blue sweater. "The shoeshine kid just came through the door and it's not into paws. Although, maybe my fluorescent pink claws could use a buff."

The shoeshine machine inched forward, its brush whirring eagerly.

"Okay, Shoe-bot. You can polish as long as I'm sitting here." While the machine happily brushed her boots, Sabrina tried to think of a cool shower gift for Aunt Vesta. She had been so busy all week she hadn't had a minute to shop. She couldn't even remember what it felt like to relax. In addition to having more homework than usual and helping Val and Hilda with the wedding preparations, Aunt Vesta had recruited her to help keep the appliances under control and on schedule. However, Aunt Vesta had miscalculated the schedule by a whole day. Consequently, with the midnight deadline only a few hours away, all the household machines were desperately trying to make up the lost time. At the moment, Aunt Hilda and Aunt Vesta were downstairs bribing the mobile ones to stay out of the living room during the bridal shower, which was due to start in thirty minutes.

"I have to conjure up a gift in a hurry, Salem. Something mortal Aunt Vesta wouldn't think of herself. Got any ideas?"

"How about a year's supply of freeze-dried seafood delicacies, which she won't think of, won't be able to use, and I'll get by default."

"I don't think so." Sabrina sighed, then started when Aunt Hilda stuck her head in the door.

"Move it, Sabrina! Val will be here any minute, and we still have to mix the punch and set out the snack trays. And I can't even sneak a point because Vesta is watching every move I make!" Hilda muttered as she turned away, "I just know I've forgotten something."

"Be right there." Sabrina stood up and flicked a point, conjuring a black espresso coffeemaker. Like all things acquired by magic, the gourmet appliance bore a label that was similar to the mortal realm brand name. "Kruds?"

"Vesta won't know the difference," Salem said. "In fact, she probably won't even know what it is."

"I hope." After wrapping the machine with another point, Sabrina picked up the gift and started for the door. The Shoe-bot whirred at her heels, and the hair dryer swooped in for another quick pass. "Don't you guys have something better to do?"

The appliances surrounded her, shaking and whirring in agitation. If they didn't keep working until midnight, they wouldn't qualify for luxury overhauls. Sabrina had no doubt that desperation might drive them downstairs, where their industrious activities might be hard to explain to Aunt Vesta's mortal guests.

"Okay, listen up. I'll give you all something to do, but you've got to promise to stay away from the party. Got it?"

The machines stood at expectant attention.

Sabrina opened her closet and pointed up twenty pairs of scuffed shoes and boots. The Shoe-bot scurried inside and went to work. Motioning the hair dryer and garage vac to follow, Sabrina grabbed a few stuffed animals off the turret window chair and escorted the machines into the bathroom. She plugged the tub, turned the water on to soak the stuffed animals, then adjusted the water to a slow, but steady, flow.

"Okay, vac. Do *not* let the tub overflow." As the garage vac dropped its hose nozzle into the tub, Sabrina set the dripping stuffed animals on the sink and turned to the hair dryer. "How are you with soggy plush?"

The dryer hovered in front of the animals and blasted them with a burst of hot air.

"Works for me!" Satisfied that the machines wouldn't disrupt the shower, Sabrina closed the bathroom door and dashed downstairs just as Vesta swept through the foyer from the den. She looked dazzling in a long, flowing black skirt and a near-sheer white blouse with a long tapered collar and billowing sleeves. She also looked upset. "What's the matter, Aunt Vesta?"

"Zelda can be so cold! I just asked her to answer the door and greet the guests while Hilda and I finish up in the kitchen, and she snapped my head off!"

Zelda leaned out the den doorway. Her blond hair looked as if it hadn't been combed in days, and she was wearing the jeans and rumpled T-shirt she had worn the day before. "In case you've forgotten, Vesta, you're getting married in eighteen hours, and I *still* haven't found the shawl!"

Vesta spun to face her, hands on her hips. "We *still* don't know how to break the spell anyway!"

Zelda grunted with exasperation and ducked back into the den out of sight.

"Spell?" Val looked up from the embossed coasters and cocktail napkins she was stacking on the coffee table in the living room. "What spell?"

"Yes, Vesta." Hilda entered from the dining room holding two crystal dishes filled with whole cashews and foil-wrapped truffles. She paused with a smug, I-knew-you'd-mess-up smile on her face. "What spell?"

"Uh, spell?" Flustered by her verbal slip in front of a mortal, Vesta experienced a total brain-crash. "Uh—"

"Bell!" Sabrina said brightly. "She said bell! Not spell. When did you get here, Val?"

"About five minutes ago." Val cocked her head. "Why would you want to break a bell?"

"Uh—tradition?" Sabrina's mind raced. "Yeah! Some people smash champagne glasses at weddings, and we break bells. Right?" She shot a desperate look at Aunt Hilda. The shower hadn't even started yet, and they were already scrambling to explain the inexplicable.

"Right! It's an old, uh—Cossack custom." Rolling her eyes, Hilda carried the snack dishes to the piano. Then she hustled Val out before Vesta blundered again. "Give me a hand with the punch, will you, Val?"

"Sure. I didn't know Sabrina was Russian—"

Sabrina sagged as Val followed Hilda into the kitchen, wondering again if she should change. Val had dressed in a short cranberry skirt with a short matching jacket over a satin tee striped in shades of brown.

"Thanks, Sabrina. Keeping a low profile around mortals isn't as easy as I thought." Aunt Vesta sighed despondently, then brightened when she noticed the wrapped box in Sabrina's arms. "Is that for me?"

"Yeah." Sabrina shoved the package into Vesta's hands. "Why don't you find a place for the gifts, and I'll take door duty. And don't worry about the slip. We all do it and covering up is an acquired art. You'll learn."

"I'm not so sure." Sighing again, Vesta left the foyer when the doorbell rang.

After checking for stray appliances, Sabrina opened the door. "Harvey!"

"Hey, Sabrina." Harvey smiled and waved shyly. "I'm here."

"Why? Not that I'm not glad to see you," Sabrina added when Harvey blinked with confusion, "but the shower is for females only."

"That's okay. I already took one today." Harvey shifted awkwardly, then walked in as Sabrina stepped back. "I guess the rental company is really particular, huh?"

"Am I supposed to know what you're talking about?"

"Is that Harvey?" Smiling warmly, Aunt Vesta swept back into the foyer and gave him an approving once-over. "My, you are a handsome fellow."

"Yeah?" Harvey blushed. "Thank you."

"Did you invite him, Aunt Vesta?" Sabrina asked.

"No, Zelda did. He has to try on his tux to make sure it fits." Taking Harvey by the arm, Vesta steered him toward the stairs. "Turn left. First door on the right. Call me when you're ready."

"Okay." Harvey bounded up the stairs two at a time.

"Wait!" Sabrina paled. "He can't—"

"Vesta!" Hilda shouted. "Your pigs in a blanket are smoking!"

"Uh-oh!" Hitching up her long skirt, Vesta bolted for the kitchen.

"But—" Sabrina started toward the stairs, then stopped when the doorbell rang again. Torn, she hesitated, then called after Harvey as she opened the door. "Don't use the bathroom!"

Sabrina's welcoming smile froze in place when she turned and saw Libby glaring at her. Wearing a loose crocheted beige sweater over a simple sea-green dress with thin shoulder straps, Libby looked great. A fine gold necklace and sandals enhanced the image of casual elegance.

I should have changed! Sabrina quelled a rush of dismay that might cue the misery-cloud to appear.

"We can't use the bathroom? I *knew* it was a bad idea to come to this lame hen party." Libby flipped her long, shining dark hair over her shoulder and tucked a small gift box under her arm.

"You're right! Bye!" Sabrina was about to slam the door closed when Aunt Zelda's frantic voice stopped her.

"Did I hear Libby?" Aunt Zelda ran out of the den, changing into belted black slacks and a blouse and styling her hair on the way to the door. "Hello, Libby! Don't you want to come in?"

"Not really. The only reason I'm here is because Mr. Kraft promised to permanently reserve a cafeteria table for the cheerleaders and athletic teams." Grimacing, she cautiously peered inside. "I'm not sure it'll be worth it."

Zelda laughed. "You do have a unique wit, don't you?"

Puzzled by Aunt Hilda's exaggerated delight, Sabrina moved aside as her aunt pulled Libby inside. She dragged the reluctant girl into the living room and brusquely pushed her down on the couch.

"Here." Aunt Zelda whipped a candy dish off the piano. "Have a truffle. I think Val's in the kitchen. She should be out soon."

"The walking definition of insecurity? Do me a favor and don't bother. Hopelessly inadequate nervous people give me indigestion." Libby took a truffle. "This little gathering isn't going to be written up on the society page of the Westbridge paper, is it?"

"No, I'm afraid not." A definitive strain crept into Zelda's voice.

"Good. All my cool friends think I'm home with the flu."

"Just sit there and don't move, okay?" Fisting her finger, Aunt Zelda walked back to Sabrina, muttering under her breath. "She's so lucky I've outgrown turning bimbos into frogs."

"*I* haven't outgrown it." Huffing, Sabrina glared at Zelda. "What was that all about?"

Before Zelda could answer, the doorbell rang again. Sabrina yanked the door open. "Yes!"

"Hello." An elderly woman smiled uncertainly. The small 1950s-style hat perched on top of gray hair pulled back in a neat bun almost fell off when she leaned forward slightly. She wore a belted print dress and clutched a handbag in front of her. "This *is* the Spellman residence, isn't it?"

Zelda recovered first. "Yes, it is. Won't you come in—"

"Mrs. Bernard Morley. Sadie will do nicely, though. My husband is head of the university history department. He's Mr. Whittier's boss." She turned to look at two women standing behind her.

Sabrina hung back watching curiously as Sadie introduced them. Crystal Hancock looked to be about forty and stood ramrod straight. Her expression was as unyielding as her stark, tailored, dark blue suit. Marla Thompson was younger, but reminded Sabrina of Agnes Gootch in the old film

Auntie Mame that Aunt Hilda watched over and over again. Wearing thick glasses and a baggy brown sweater over a shapeless mid-calf plaid skirt, Ash's research assistant had her dark hair pulled back in a severe twist. Marla gave Sabrina a fleeting smile as she filed in behind the others.

"Like mixing oil and water," Sabrina whispered as Aunt Zelda escorted them into the living room. She wasn't quite ready to exchange fire with Libby, but Vesta, Hilda, and Val joined the group before Libby insulted the odd mix of newcomers.

"Pssst! Sabrina!" Harvey stood at the top of the stairs, looking totally hunk in a gray tuxedo that fit him perfectly. He was shoeless and lifted one of his feet. Water dripped off his sopping wet sock. "The hall's flooded up here. I didn't know if I should go into the bathroom to check, since you told me not to use it."

"Uh, well—" Sabrina winced. The garage vac obviously wasn't doing its job, but she couldn't let Harvey investigate the problem. Vacuum cleaners and hair dryers didn't function on their own at his house. "Okay. I'm coming."

"Where are you going?" Aunt Zelda grabbed Sabrina's arm. "We've got to talk. Now!"

"But I left the water running in the bathroom!" Sabrina glanced upward. "I sort of left the garage vac and the hair dryer running, too."

"More easily fixed than our other problems." Aunt Zelda pointed up the stairs to turn off the tap and spotted Harvey. "Oh, good. You're here. Take that tux off and put your shoes on! And hurry!"

"Okay." Harvey shrugged and wiggled his toes. "But my socks are wet!"

Zelda waved Sabrina into the den and cast another quick point up the stairs.

"Hey! What do you know?" Harvey laughed. "They're dry already."

"Aunt Zelda!" Sabrina hissed.

"If he asks, just tell him his mom must have bought the newest thing in wash-and-wear! Now, come on." Aunt Zelda rushed ahead of Sabrina. "We're running out of time."

Suddenly worried, Sabrina ran after her. "Please, don't tell me you can't find the shawl."

"I won't." Sliding into her desk chair, Zelda moved her computer mouse. Her OR version of a popular screensaver disengaged to reveal a topographical map of Central Europe. The aerial view zoomed in on a forest surrounded by high mountains. "Gertrude's got the shawl in her castle, which is right down there somewhere."

"Somewhere? That's a hundred square miles!"

Zelda nodded glumly. "That's as close as Gertrude's private protection wards would let me get electronically."

"But how are you going to get the *shawl* if you don't know exactly where it is?"

"I'm not." Zelda looked up slowly. "You and Libby and Harvey are."

Chapter 12

"What?" Sabrina shook her head, convinced she had misunderstood Aunt Zelda. "You didn't mean that Harvey and Libby and I have to go get the shawl in person, did you?"

"That's exactly what I meant." Zelda slumped back in her chair. "Only the youngest licensed witch in the family—you—and your true love—"

"Harvey." Sabrina sighed. "He's even certified."

"—and your romantic rival can find and escape with the shawl. I stumbled across that information on an obscure web site yesterday." Zelda frowned. "Libby still has designs on Harvey, doesn't she?"

"As my luck would have it, yeah." Sabrina started, filled with sudden anxiety. "Wait a minute. 'Escape'? As in run for your life?"

"I don't know." Standing up, Zelda held Sabrina

by the arms and looked her in the eye. "But I do know you can do it."

"But how do we convince Harvey and Libby to do it?" Harvey might go along, but she couldn't imagine Libby agreeing to an impromptu hike through a European forest on a wild-shawl chase. What a disaster!

"I've got an idea—" Zelda jerked back, her gaze darting upward.

Sabrina groaned when she glanced up and saw the misery-cloud. "Great! Now what do I do?"

"Pretend it isn't there. Trust me." Zelda pointed up a dish of truffles that was identical to the one in the living room. "Make sure Harvey eats one of these. I'll get Libby."

"Right. It wouldn't be fair to pop him out to an uncertain fate on an empty stomach." As Zelda hurried into the living room, Sabrina waited in the doorway and called Harvey when he came down the stairs. "Harvey! Over here. I've got a problem and I need your help."

"It doesn't involve anything weird, does it?" Harvey stopped suddenly, staring.

"Weird? What's your definition?" Sabrina asked casually.

"Well, weird like that dark cloud hanging over your head."

"What cloud?" Sabrina glanced upward and shrugged. "I don't see a cloud."

"You don't?" Harvey shook his head. "Now, *that* is weird. I have some pretty bizarre dreams sometimes, but this is the first time it's happened while I was awake."

"What kind of dreams?" Sabrina's eyes narrowed. Like Val, Harvey could be a little dense. Right now, it was definitely an asset.

"Falling into bottomless vortexes. Sword fighting with short guys in funny hats. Stuff like that."

"Uh-huh." Sabrina grabbed his hand and hauled him into the den. "Here. Have a truffle."

"Thanks." Taking a handful of foil-wrapped candies, Harvey leaned over to watch rows of winged toasters float across the computer screen. "Did you know there's mail popping out of these toasters."

"It's a special order version." Thunder boomed through the house, and Sabrina dashed to the doorway as Gail Kipling trotted down the stairs. She had completely forgotten they had invited her father's Other Realm girlfriend and that she'd be arriving via the linen closet. "Better than *sparkling* in from the book by the piano."

In the living room Val and the mortal women were looking around with puzzled expressions. Vesta and Hilda exchanged startled glances.

Gail greeted Zelda in the foyer as she hustled by with Libby in tow. "Sorry I'm late, Zelda. I got held up in court. The Wizard of Ooze made fun of Drell's mole in public again, and he pressed charges. It got a little messy."

Libby's nose wrinkled in disgust. "Isn't anyone around here normal?"

Gail raised an eyebrow and a finger. "How would you like to spend a little time on a lily pad?"

"Did Mother change her mind about coming?" Zelda asked.

"No," Gail said. "She sends her condolences."

"Vesta and Hilda are in the living room, Gale. Excuse me." Zelda dragged Libby out of harm's way and into the den, closing the door behind them.

"Okay. What's the big emergency?" Furious, Libby crossed her arms and scowled at Aunt Zelda. Her frown deepened when her gaze settled on Sabrina's misery-cloud. "There's a cloud over your head."

"No, there's not," Sabrina said.

"What cloud?" Aunt Zelda's eyes widened slightly.

"Now, that's really weird, Libby." Harvey unwrapped another truffle. "We're both seeing the same things that aren't there."

"Harvey!" Libby spun around. "What are you doing here?"

"Eating truffles."

"Truffles!" Inhaling sharply, Aunt Zelda slapped her hand to her face. "No wonder!"

A little slow on the uptake, it took Sabrina a few seconds to realize her aunt was setting up a cover story to explain the impending side-trip.

"What?" Libby's expression reflected a rare moment of uncertainty. *"I* ate one of those truffles."

Harvey swallowed. "I ate six."

"They're not dangerous," Zelda said. "The regular truffles got switched with some I made to test an experimental imagination amplifier I've been developing."

Libby gasped. "You used us as guinea pigs?"

"No, it was an accident. The amplifier is completely harmless." Zelda held out her hand in a placating gesture, disguising the points she cast at each of them. "You're just going to get very tired and fall asleep. And you might have some vivid dreams before you wake up in a couple of hours."

"A couple of—" Libby's head flopped sideways as she fell sound asleep on her feet.

Harvey's eyes snapped closed, and his chin dropped to his chest. He started snoring.

"Not bad, Aunt Zelda. Now what?"

Zelda moved the computer mouse to reveal the overhead view of the forest. "Concentrate on the screen and pick a spot that feels right. Maybe you'll get lucky and pop in close to the castle."

Nodding, Sabrina stared at the green canopy of distant treetops displayed on the screen. She couldn't make out any details, but one area in the northwest corner drew her attention. "Here's goes nothing. . . ."

Keeping her eyes on the chosen spot, Sabrina chanted.

"Harvey and Libby, come with me
to find a castle in those trees."

With a snap of her fingers, Sabrina instantaneously transported herself and her unsuspecting team into a small, woodland glen cloaked in darkness. The thick tangle of tree branches overhead blocked out the moon and stars. Pointing up a lantern, Sabrina took a quick look around to get her bearings. Strangely shaped toadstools grew among patches of withered grass. The surrounding forest was pitch black.

"I've got a really bad feeling about this." Sabrina shivered as the misery-cloud spattered her with cold drops of water.

"You're not the only one." Harvey held his hand above his eyes to peer into the blanket of night.

"How'd we get outside?" Libby shuddered and pulled her lightweight sweater closed.

"We didn't," Sabrina said lightly. "It's all in your mind."

"Then how come I'm freezing?" Libby whined.

"Because you have an overactive imagination?" Feeling as if she was being watched, Sabrina held the lantern high to scan the darkness.

"I'm imagining a welcoming committee," Harvey said.

"Me, too!" Sabrina laughed nervously as four wizened trolls stepped into the circle of light, surrounding them on all sides. Bearded and wearing medieval palace guard costumes, they crossed their stubby arms and glared at the intruders.

"They cannot possibly be a figment of *my* imagination." Libby waved a hand and shook her head, rejecting what she assumed was an illusion. "I don't dream ugly, little creeps."

"Be warned and hold that wagging tongue—" The troll in the red hat bristled.

"—or be catching flies with a forked one!" The troll wearing a blue hat finished.

Sabrina perked up at the poetic reference to the childish turn-a-bimbo-into-a-frog spell. That was the kind of thing a vindictive witch like Gertrude wouldn't outgrow. After all, she had been hiding the spinster shawl and pouting for a thousand years!

"And pray, what be ye doing here—" Yellow hat squinted suspiciously.

Green hat completed the rhyme. "Where none dare tread without a fear?"

"Actually, we're looking for Gertrude's castle," Sabrina said.

"In *your* nightmare!" Libby snarled. "Not mine."

Sabrina ignored her, her attention on the trolls. "Do you know where it is?"

The four trolls nodded vigorously.

"Okay, where?"

Blue hat held up a staying finger, then drew his companions into a conference huddle. Red hat was elected to speak for the group.

"Removing the Wards will reveal where Gertrude's castle is concealed."

"Can you give me a hint?" If Aunt Zelda with all her centuries of experience couldn't remove the magical protective wards, how was she supposed to do it?

Blue hat shook his head. Red hat rolled his eyes upward. Green hat jiggled nervously, and yellow hat dug his toe into the dirt. All of them gave the impression they wanted to tell, but couldn't. Or didn't dare.

"I've never been out of these woods," red hat said.

"But we'd love to leave, if we *could.*" Blue hat held her gaze intently.

"I see." Hoping she understood, Sabrina asked, "And where would you like to go."

"A Caribbean cruise would be stunning—" Yellow hat sighed wistfully.

"As long as Gertrude's not coming!" Green hat frowned.

"No problem!" Sabrina pointed packed suitcases into the trolls' hands and replaced their guard costumes with flowered shirts and Bermuda shorts. *"Bon voyage!"* She pointed again.

Smiling and waving, the trolls popped out. Sabrina picked up the business card that floated to the ground and read it by lantern light. "'Castle Security, Unlimited. Sebastian, Donald, Charley, and Gregory Ward.' Cool!"

Harvey stared at the ground, then looked up laughing. "Oh! Now I get it. Remove the *Wards!* I never knew my imagination had a sense of humor."

Sabrina shoved the card in her pocket, then noticed a muted glow filtering through the trees ahead. "I think the castle's that way. Are you two coming?"

"Yeah." Harvey nodded enthusiastically. "I can't wait to see what I think up next."

"Not a chance," Libby said. "I'm going to imagine myself *out* of this juvenile adventure game."

"Suit yourself." Leading the way with the lantern held high, Sabrina started toward the trees. She stumbled when the high heels on her boots sank into the soft ground. Exchanging them for a pair of low-heeled hiking boots, she turned her finger on the bushes and low tree branches to clear a path through the forest.

"That cloud is still hanging over you, Sabrina," Harvey said. "I think it likes you."

"It's a symbiotic relationship. Misery loves company." The thing was, Sabrina realized, she wasn't nearly as miserable as she had been when the cloud had first attached to her. In fact, aside from the stakes being so high, she was almost enjoying herself. If she didn't lose the cloud to someone else soon, the bond would be so strong nothing short of constant mindless hysteria would make it go away.

A ferocious roar shattered the silence in the woods behind them. Libby screamed, then snapped brittle brush and branches as she plunged into the woods to catch up.

"Wait for meeeeee!"

Sabrina stopped and smiled, wondering if things were going as well at Aunt Vesta's bridal shower.

* * *

Hilda sat with a smile frozen on her face and a snack plate perched on her knee, trying to look interested as Sadie finished telling a story about her daughter's wedding.

"Well, the phone started ringing off the hook," Sadie said.

Crystal's shoulders rose and fell with a bored sigh. She had obviously heard the story many times before. Marla, on the other hand, was listening with rapt fascination. Val and Vesta both fidgeted, watching the time. Gail wandered back in from her eighth trip to the refreshment table in the dining room. Hilda checked a twinge of envy, wondering how the slim woman could eat so much and not gain an ounce.

"Everyone was driving around town, wondering if we had given them the wrong directions to the hotel." Sadie took a sip of punch and giggled.

"Pssst." Salem stuck his head out from under the couch, where he had been hiding since shortly after the party began. Not that Hilda blamed him. He looked ridiculous with no fur. "Pass me another one of those clamshell things, please."

Hilda met Vesta's quizzical gaze as she took a crab-stuffed clamshell off her plate and held it over the end of the couch. Salem grabbed it in his teeth and ducked back into hiding. A few seconds later she heard a crunching sound. Salem was giving the inedible shells to the mini-vac.

"The hotel management hadn't bothered to tell us that the place had been sold and a *different* sign was going up that day!" Laughing, Sadie wiped tears from her eyes. "Can you imagine?"

"Not in my wildest dreams," Hilda said flatly.

"I thought it was a charming story, Sadie," Zelda said.

"Is that kind of inconsiderate incompetence pervasive in the mortal world?" Vesta asked.

Sadie blinked. "I beg your pardon, dear?"

"Uh, I just meant—" Vesta took a deep breath, then patted Sadie's hand. "How thoughtless of them."

"Inexcusable." Gail nodded. "It's no different in the OR, though."

Sadie glanced at Gail sympathetically. "Have you had bad experiences with surgery, too?"

Val looked at Zelda. "How long does it take to get more crackers? Sabrina's been gone over an hour. Aren't you worried?"

"Yes!" Zelda, Hilda, and Vesta answered simultaneously.

"I'm sure she's just fine," Hilda added lamely. In truth, she was very concerned. It had taken Zelda a whole week just to *find* the shawl because Gertrude was an old, cunning, and powerful witch, who knew all the tricks of the craft and took her grudges way too seriously. Sabrina and her mortal friends didn't have much of a chance against her and there was no telling how Gertrude would react to the challenge.

Val set her plate aside. "I'm going to check on Libby."

"No!" Zelda bolted upright and smiled tightly. "I really think it's better if we just let her sleep. I had no idea chocolate gave her such severe headaches."

"Yeah, maybe you're right." Val sighed. "She already hates me. Waking her up to throbbing agony probably wouldn't win me any points. Not that I care! I don't—most of the time. I mean, there's a lot more to high school than being cool and popular and off Libby's verbal hit list—"

Gail stuffed a carrot stick in Val's mouth. "Will it matter a century from now?"

Val shook her head.

Hilda passed Salem another clamshell, then noticed the subplot developing by the piano.

Marla fumbled her plate, almost spilling it when Vesta caught her staring. She smiled, shyly. "I, I didn't mean to be rude, Vesta. It's just that— you're so beautiful and witty and sophisticated. I'm not surprised Professor Whittier fell in love with you just like that."

"How sweet." Vesta shifted to face the plain young woman. "Have you worked for Ash long?"

"Five years." Marla's smile tightened as she nervously averted her gaze.

Crystal eyed Vesta with undisguised disapproval, creating an uneasy tension that put everyone on edge.

Hilda opened her mouth to suggest that Vesta open her gifts. Salem's voice came out.

"Give that back, you greedy little sweep! I'm not done with it yet!"

Eight pairs of incredulous eyes watched as the mini-vac zipped out from under the couch. A clamshell was stuck in its plastic jaws, and it zoomed for the kitchen with a bald, black cat in furious pursuit.

"See if I give you any scraps again!" Salem shouted.

"Aren't these new, interactive toys astonishing?" Hilda asked brightly.

Chapter 13

☆

☆

Not much of a castle, is it?" Harvey pushed a vine back and stepped under it to stand in the glow cast by Sabrina's lantern. He looked disappointed, which wasn't hard to understand. The castle wasn't what she had expected, either.

Torches flickered on either side of a heavy wooden door with massive metal hinges and a pull ring. However, the door was set into the crumbling mortar and stones of a small windowless hovel. Which, Sabrina reminded herself, didn't necessarily mean the hovel *was* a hovel. Of the many things she had learned since finding out she was a witch, she knew that outward appearances could be deceiving with things magical.

"I'm going to sue your aunt, Sabrina." Libby stumbled out of the woods. "For emotional anguish and damage to personal property."

"Okay." Sabrina didn't take the threat seriously. No one in the mortal world would accept the existence of an imagination amplifier that resulted in torn stockings, mud-caked sandals, and a ruined manicure. The twigs and leaves clinging to Libby's sweater and hair could be removed, and if the cheerleader didn't antagonize Aunt Zelda, she might pay the dry-cleaning bill for the dirty, wrinkled dress. Besides, if Libby hadn't been trailing so far behind in a petulant snit, she wouldn't have had to fight her way through the woods.

"Should we go inside?" Harvey asked.

"Might as well." Sabrina studied the door, looking for anything that might be a booby trap. "I'm just not sure how to get through the door."

"I don't *want* to go through the door." Libby fumed.

Before Sabrina could stop him, Harvey stepped forward and pulled the metal ring. She cringed, expecting some terrible consequence.

The door swung open with an eerie *creeeeak*.

A swarm of alarm lizards didn't scurry out, and they weren't suddenly stricken with forty-eight-hour itch mold.

"Way!" Sabrina lowered the lantern to rest her arm. Harvey had the mortal advantage of not knowing he might be walking into a witch's trap.

"I've been thinking about what Libby said back in the clearing." Harvey stepped into the darkened doorway. "About this being like an adventure game."

"What about it?" Sabrina asked.

"Well, it's almost *exactly* like the role-playing adventures I was hooked on back in junior high. Which makes sense since we're all in my imagination, right?"

"Unfortunately," Libby snapped, picking leaves out of her snarled hair.

"Yeah, sort of." Sabrina cocked her head. "Why?"

"Well, then"—Harvey paused, staring into an interior darkness that seemed endless—"there must be something we have to do to win the game!"

"That seems logical." Sabrina smiled, sensing Harvey's excitement. He was making this too easy, but she wasn't going to complain—or explain. He probably wouldn't understand what the big deal was about a cursed shawl, and Libby wouldn't care.

"Then let's do whatever it is so we can get out of here!" Libby pushed past them through the door and immediately became invisible in the inky blackness. "The light, Sabrina!"

Harvey picked up the lantern and took Sabrina by the hand. "This is too cool, Sabrina. Come on!"

"Cool" wasn't how Sabrina would describe it, and her doubts about completing her mission intensified when they stepped through the door. As she had anticipated, the outside of Gertrude's stronghold was a façade, disguising the true nature of the castle.

"Wow!" Harvey's eyes sparkled as the lantern's glow expanded to light up an enormous chamber.

"Oh, gross!" Libby grimaced.

Sabrina's spirits sank suddenly. The misery-cloud above her wasn't thrilled, either. It rumbled, sweating raindrops of distress.

Made of rough-hewn stone, the walls rose fifty feet high, then angled to form a higher peaked ceiling. Huge beams crisscrossed the open space where walls and ceiling joined, and a few large, tattered tapestries hung from the rafters. There were no windows. Numerous flights of stone steps—straight, curved, and spiraled—led down into a central pit. Other steps wound up along the walls. Some of them came to an abrupt end suspended over the pit. Others ended at the wall. There were piles of junk everywhere: tarnished armor, rusted swords, dented shields, broken wheels, black kettles, and various corked bottles. Everything was covered with dirt and sheets of cobwebs. Hundreds of glittering eyes stared down at them from recesses in the stone. On the floor below, a carved, wooden throne sat on a raised platform in front of a cauldron hanging over a fire-pit. Two vultures perched on the back of the throne.

"Nobody sane thinks up something like this, Harvey," Libby said.

"I can't take all the credit." Harvey shrugged. "This looks a lot like the fortress in Ancient Ghost Hunters."

"If we were in *my* head, we'd be bargain hunting! What's that?" Libby looked down, squealed, and kicked, flinging a small green snake off her foot. It landed in a pile of rags and slithered away into the folds.

Sabrina picked up a long stick and carefully poked through the shredded fabrics, but the black shawl wasn't there.

"I'm going to look around." Setting the lantern on a stone pedestal, Harvey cautiously moved down a flight of steps leading into the pit.

"I'll go with you," Sabrina said.

"Can't you imagine some heat, Harvey?" Libby complained as she followed close behind.

When they reached the bottom of the stairs, Harvey aimlessly wandered about looking at everything with idle curiosity. Sabrina conducted a systematic search for the shawl.

"It's colder in here than it was outside." Libby's teeth chattered.

Arctic, Sabrina thought, waving a finger over her velour tee to add a layer of insulation. Libby moved closer to the stone fire-pit to warm up. The coals were still hot, which meant that Gertrude hadn't been gone long and could return without warning any time.

The shrill shriek of a falcon echoed off the stone walls.

Like now!

"Everybody down!" Sabrina shouted as a huge predatory bird flew off a ceiling beam and swooped down on them.

"Now what?" Libby whined, but hit the deck and threw her arms over her head.

Harvey ducked, pulling Sabrina down beside him. The trembling misery-cloud wrapped itself around her shoulders.

The falcon screeched as it circled, barely missing their heads with its talons before it landed on the throne. The screech became a cackle as the bird transformed into a shriveled old witch with dry, wrinkled skin and long, scraggly gray hair. A tattered black shawl was draped around her scrawny frame.

"Took you long enough, missy." Gertrude's steely black eyes bore into Sabrina. "I thought one of you Spellman girls would have been here centuries ago to get the spinster shawl."

Sabrina stood up and calmly brushed herself off. She wasn't about to admit it had taken her genius aunt and the wonders of modern technology to track Gertrude down. "We've been a little busy the past thousand years."

"Wallowing in unhappiness, no doubt. That's the sorriest misery-cloud I've ever seen." Gertrude cackled again. "The boyfriend isn't exactly a knight in shining armor, either, is he?"

"I like him," Sabrina said defensively.

Libby stood up and groaned. Her hand was covered with purple goo of unknown origins. She wiped the icky stuff off on a rag hanging on a nearby hook. The rag gagged, then flew away. "Okay, Harvey. Enough is enough. Cut!"

"Ooh, I like *her!*" Gertrude wagged her bony finger at Libby. "You've got a bit of a mean streak, too, don'cha?"

"You think?" Rolling her eyes, Libby sidled closer to Harvey.

"So I'll just take our shawl now." Sabrina didn't see any reason to beat around the bush. She pointed to yank the grungy, torn covering away from Gertrude, but the shawl stubbornly clung to the old woman's shoulders.

"You can't take it unless I let go of it." Gertrude drew the shawl tighter and clutched it closed with a bent, knobby hand. "And I will, if you give him"— she pointed at Harvey, then shifted her finger to Libby—"to her. But be warned! You won't be getting him back. Once the bargain is sealed, it can't be broken."

"Harvey!" Libby brightened, assuming the old hag's request was really an expression of Harvey's subconscious desire.

"I don't think so." Sabrina raised her finger to give the old witch a nasty dose of scalp itch. She planned to grab the shawl the instant Gertrude let go to scratch.

Gertrude was a split second faster and lobbed a finger snafu at Sabrina. Resembling an old-fashioned wooden clothespin, the snafu was designed to muffle a finger, preventing any magic from being released. Reacting on reflex, Sabrina ducked and the snafu clamped onto Libby's nose.

Squealing, Libby closed her eyes. "This isn't really happening. This isn't really happening—"

Realizing it was attached to a mortal nose and not a magic finger, the snafu unclamped and rocketed away, spitting in disgust.

"Where am I getting all this stuff?" Oblivious to the seriousness of the situation, Harvey rocked back on his heels and grinned.

Sabrina countered with a narrow-beam hurricane spell, hoping to whip the shawl off Gertrude's shoulders.

Gertrude just cackled and waved the windy blast aside.

Desperate, Sabrina braced herself and wished she had paid a little more attention to the dueling fingers chapter when she had been studying for her witch's license. Gertrude had a thousand years more experience and she was definitely out*witched.* But—not necessarily out*witted!*

Spinning around, Sabrina pointed at the fire-pit. Blazing flames erupted, raising the temperature in the frigid room eighty degrees in a split second.

Taken by surprise, Gertrude let go of the shawl to fan herself with her hand. Sabrina snagged it with another point before it hit the floor.

"Run!" Motioning Libby and Harvey to move out ahead of her, Sabrina bolted back up the stairs.

"You can't get away from me!" Gertrude screamed.

Sabrina glanced back to see tongues of fire lapping at her heels. Gertrude cackled hysterically as she raised her arms to unleash her ancient magic to stop their escape.

"Thank you so much for coming!" Vesta bid Sadie, Crystal, and Marla goodbye. She stood between the doorjamb and the edge of the front door, which was partially closed to block their view of the foyer. With just over an hour to go before midnight, Hilda and Zelda were fighting a losing battle with every appliance in the house. Pretending to have something in her eye, Gail had locked herself in the downstairs bathroom with Val until they had the mutiny under control.

"It was a lovely party, Vesta!" Sadie smiled as she shuffled toward the steps.

"I'll see you all tomorrow!" Just when Vesta thought the three mortal women were finally leaving, Sadie turned and started back.

"Can you tell me where to get one of those robot duster-upper contraptions? I have back problems and—"

"I'll ask Zelda and let you know tomorrow. Promise." Vesta smiled back, but her thoughts were less than civil. *Now go away!*

"You'll be such a beautiful bride." Sadie paused, sighing.

"Not if I don't get my beauty sleep." Vesta spoke through gritted teeth. She couldn't be rude because Sadie's husband was Ash's boss. Turning the sweet, well-meaning but exasperating old lady into a giant clam wasn't an option, either. Not for a make-believe mortal whose immediate future depended on her new husband's job security.

"Oh, my, yes! It's been so long since Bernie and I were married, I'd forgotten that I couldn't sleep the—"

"Better run before Crystal and Marla leave without you." When Sadie looked away, Vesta slammed the door and stormed into the dining room. Hilda was dumping the leftover snacks on the floor. The carper shampooer, vacuum cleaner, and mini-vac attacked the mess like bluefish in a feeding frenzy. "Where's Zelda?"

"Upstairs flooding the bathroom for the garage vac. It only needs another half hour to qualify." After pointing the dirty platters and bowls into the dishwasher, Hilda pointed the machine on. "There. I think we've got everyone covered."

Exhausted, Vesta trudged back into the living room behind Hilda and collapsed on the couch. She grunted a greeting when Zelda flopped down beside her.

"If my calculations are correct," Zelda said wearily, "all the appliances will make their work-hour quota by eleven fifty-six."

"I certainly hope so." Hilda sat in the armchair and used her finger to collect the discarded napkins and paper plates into a pile. "I don't think I could stand having them all moping around the house for the next year."

"I'm worried about Sabrina." Leaning forward,

Vesta propped her elbows on her knees and rested her chin on clasped hands. "I should have looked for the shawl years ago or just kept the secret and taken my chances with Ash."

Zelda tried to console her. "You didn't know that the youngest licensed witch in the family had to go, Vesta."

"True, but maybe we shouldn't have sent her after you found out, Zelda."

Yeah." Hilda sighed. "It's not like I couldn't get *used* to being unlucky in love. I've had six hundred years of practice."

"Sabrina is very resourceful. I'm sure she'll be fine." Zelda paused. "Pretty sure."

Vesta stared at the growing pile of trash on the floor. Her stomach felt hollow and her heart ached. She had never experienced profound guilt before and she didn't like it. When she had realized that Marla was secretly in love with Ash, she had felt a twinge of sympathy, but that was a minor irritation compared to what she'd feel if anything terrible happened to Sabrina.

"Open wide, trash guy!" Hilda yelled. "Another load coming at ya!" Waving her hand, she sent a stream of trash zooming toward the kitchen and the seemingly bottomless trash compactor.

Someone screamed.

"Uh-oh." Gail stopped dead as she entered the living room from the foyer.

Pale and shaken, Val staggered in from the dining

room. "Did you see that?" She looked back over her shoulder as the tail end of the trash stream disappeared into the kitchen.

"What?" All four witches answered.

"The napkins and plates. They just flew by—"

Zelda stood up and put an arm around Val's shoulders. "You didn't happen to eat any truffles, did you?"

Val nodded, then gasped as Sabrina, Harvey, and Libby suddenly appeared by the piano.

"I got it!" Laughing, Sabrina jumped up and down, waving a filthy, torn black cloth over her head. The misery-cloud hovered higher to avoid being smacked.

Vesta clamped a hand to her chest, overwhelmed with relief. "You're back! And safe!"

Harvey grinned at Zelda. "That imagination amplifier is worth a fortune!"

"Thank you, Harvey, but I don't think the world is quite ready for it yet." Zelda glanced at Libby.

Looking as tattered, torn, and dirty as the shawl, Libby stood in a dazed stupor—until something tangled in her hair began to flap. Her eyes widened and her mouth fell open in horror. "Bats! I've got bats in my hair!"

Sabrina shrugged. "I guess we didn't outrun them all before I finally remembered to *pop* us out of Gertrude's castle."

"Get them off!" Libby frantically shook her head, afraid to shoo the trapped creatures away with her hands. "Get them off!"

"Calm down. They're not real, remember?" Zelda pointed, sending the bats back where they came from. "See?"

"They looked real." Val's voice quivered. "Just like that cloud hanging over Sabrina."

"You must have eaten truffles, too." Harvey glanced at Zelda with a mischievous twinkle in his eye. "Could I have a doggie bag?"

As Libby's breathing slowed, fury edged out disgust and terror. "I have never been so *miserable* in my whole life!"

Woooooooshhhhhhh!

"And now it's hanging over Libby." Val blinked as the cloud rained on the stunned cheerleader. "I think I'd better sit down."

"I'm going home!" Turning on her muddy heels, Libby stalked out the door, taking the misery-cloud with her.

"Bye," Sabrina said softly, handing Vesta the shawl. "I know this is going to sound totally insane, but in a weird way I'm going to miss the little drip. But—I'll get over it!"

"You will." Vesta glanced at the stricken girl beside her. "But I'm not so sure about Val."

"She'll be fine. I'll handle it." Sabrina took Val's arm and gently urged her to stand up. Then she leaned over to whisper to Vesta. "She ate truffles, right?"

Vesta nodded.

Worn out from all the chaos, Vesta sat quietly while Hilda left to check the status of the household appliances. Sabrina helped Harvey take Val to his car after Zelda assured him that the nonexistent effects of the made-up imagination amplifier had worn off and it was safe to drive.

Gail wandered in from the dining room. "Anyone want cake?"

"Me!" Salem leaped out of the cold fireplace where he had taken refuge, then froze. "Is it midnight yet?"

"Not yet," Zelda said, "but I've got the cat groomer locked in my closet. I hate to tell you this, Salem, but that machine didn't *have* a 'work incentive' clause. Hilda bought it from a disreputable linen closet salesman and didn't get a purchase agreement!"

"What! You mean, I've been tortured all week for nothing?"

Gail picked up the sobbing cat. "Come on, Salem. Let's go raid the refrigerator."

When Zelda ran upstairs to dismantle the cat groomer, Vesta leaned back and studied the ugly black shawl that had caused so much trouble. Sabrina's magical trip to retrieve it with her friends had put a sizable dent in her confidence. The mortal world was full of mortals! What had made her think that she could possibly keep her magical powers a secret?

Or survive without using them.

Chapter 14

☆

☆

Sabrina!" Aunt Vesta called in a panic from the bathroom.

"Coming!" Sabrina stole another look in the mirror, smoothing the empire-cut blue dress with lace trim. A cascade of small blue flowers and ribbon streamers had been woven into the hair clipped high on her head. The look was a little too frilly for her tastes, but ideal for a wedding.

"Wait a minute!" Salem called as Sabrina headed out the door. "What about me?"

"Oops! Sorry!" Sabrina pointed over her shoulder, quick-growing Salem's sleek coat of black hair.

"Thank you. The perfect end to the worst week of my life. Well, almost the worst week. Being changed into a cat rates only slightly higher than being manicured, primped, permed, shaved, and perfumed, though."

"I'm having a nervous breakdown here, Sabrina!" Aunt Vesta sounded close to tears.

"Gotta go, Salem." Sabrina dashed out and paused on the landing when she heard Hilda and Zelda arguing.

"If we twine these flower garlands around every post on the banister, we won't be finished until Monday!" Hilda snapped.

"If we don't, it'll look terrible," Zelda countered.

"I've got news for you, Zelda." Hilda sighed. "It looks terrible anyway."

That was too true. Yards of the beautiful full garland the florist had delivered had been mashed, broken, and tangled by her aunts' efforts. The untouched garland on the floor had wilted from sheer terror.

Sabrina hoped Val arrived soon. They desperately needed the help in the kitchen, and she wanted to make sure Val wasn't permanently traumatized after last night. She wasn't too worried. Harvey had believed the preposterous imagination amplifier story and had probably convinced Val before he dropped her off at her house.

Aunt Vesta, on the other hand, was falling apart, a sight Sabrina had never expected to see. She stood in front of the bathroom mirror in a robe. Dripping wet hair soaked the terry cloth over her shoulders, and black streaks of mascara ran down her cheeks. Pressing her lips together, Vesta turned on the hair dryer. The stream of lukewarm air that came out was so weak it wouldn't fluff a butterfly's wings. Vesta turned off the dryer, dropped it on the counter, and hung her head.

"Need some help?" Sabrina didn't mention that mortals put their makeup on *after* they took a shower.

"It's hopeless." Vesta sighed. "I'll never learn how to do anything the mortal way, especially under pressure."

"Don't be so hard on yourself, Aunt Vesta. You've been relying on magic for centuries. Realistically, no one could adjust to *not* using those powers in one week. Honest."

"I suppose you're right." Vesta smiled, then laughed as she caught sight of herself in the mirror. "I guess it wouldn't hurt to resort to magic this once, since it's a special occasion."

Sabrina tried to wipe some of the mascara off Vesta's face with a washcloth. The streaks just smeared. "I don't think you've got any choice."

"I was hoping you'd say that." Brandishing her finger, Vesta pointed her hair and robe dry and the makeup gone. "Now I can create from the basics up."

"Great. Aunt Zelda has your dress laid out in her bedroom with the shawl. Too bad you've got to wear that filthy old thing over that gorgeous gown." Sabrina shuddered.

"I can handle *wearing* the shawl, but beyond that, I have no idea how to break the spell."

"Maybe that's all you have to do. Wear it and hope no one steals the groom!" Sabrina joked, but she was worried about the grim future they'd all face if the spinster spell wasn't broken. And to make matters worse, Zelda would have to explain why Hilda was doing jester-time in Drell's Council Chambers whenever she insulted him!

"Maybe." Vesta smiled warmly. "Thanks for everything you did to get the shawl back, Sabrina. Gertrude didn't make things too difficult, did she?"

Sabrina shook her head. "Being chased by fire and bats gave me a few bad moments, but it was worth it to keep Harvey."

"Keep him?" Vesta frowned. "What do you mean?"

"Gertrude would have given me the shawl, but only if I had given Harvey to Libby—forever. Wasn't gonna happen."

"Sabrina!" Zelda yelled up the stairs. "We could use an extra finger down here!"

"Okay!" Sabrina turned back to Vesta. "Don't forget you're not supposed to see Ash before the ceremony. Stay up here until Dad comes. When Libby starts singing, that's your cue to start down the stairs—if Libby shows up!"

"Why wouldn't she?" Vesta asked curiously.

"Seriously? She's got the misery-cloud!"

"Not a problem. Misery-clouds don't stick to mortals for more than a few hours. It was probably gone when she woke up this morning."

"Rats." Sabrina frowned, then shrugged. "Just as well, I guess. The misery-cloud was annoying, but even it doesn't deserve to be stuck with Libby."

"Any time, Sabrina!" Zelda yelled again.

Leaving Vesta to get dressed, Sabrina hurried down the stairs. The banister and supporting posts were festooned with lush, fresh garland. A white arch entwined with identical garland stood at the base of the staircase. Apparently, Aunt Hilda and Aunt Zelda had resorted to magic out of desperation, too. Zelda was standing in the living room deciding what to point where next.

"The banister looks great, Aunt Zelda. What do you want me to do?"

Frowning thoughtfully, Zelda flicked her finger at the piano. It turned white. "Too much?"

"A little hard to explain to everyone who was here last night."

"Good point." Zelda pointed the piano back to its usual color. "Would you mind cleaning the carpet in the dining room? The floor cleaners hadn't finished when the clock struck twelve last night."

"Why do I have to do it?" Sabrina protested. "Did their motors burn out or what?"

"*All* the appliances are so exhausted after last night's work marathon, none of them will do anything this morning." Zelda exhaled, exasperated. "So you get the carpets, Sabrina. I've got to move the furniture before Willard arrives with the rental chairs."

"But—"

"Then you can help Hilda finish up in the kitchen before Val gets here. We'll never be ready in time if we don't use magic, and I don't think Val will buy truffles as an excuse again." Zelda pointed at the couch, instantly transporting it into the dungeon.

"All right, but I'm already dressed to party!" Raising her finger, Sabrina stomped into the dining room to do the dirty work.

Sabrina zapped up another platter of boiled shrimp with three varieties of sauces and steeled herself against Salem's pleas. He looked way too cute in his white tuxedo bow tie and cummerbund, and the guests wouldn't be able to resist his feline begging techniques.

"Just a few more. So my stomach doesn't growl during the ceremony."

"No, Salem. A few more shrimp and you'll bust out of your cummerbund."

"No, I won't. It's elastic in back." The cat shut up as Val bounced back in to get another platter.

"This is the last one, Val." Sabrina slipped out of her apron and tossed it on the counter.

"Everything looks great! You guys must have started working before dawn to get it all done. Mr. Kraft and Harvey are almost finished setting up the chairs." Val picked up the tray. "I did notice you're not serving truffles."

"Not unless we need them."

Val blanked, then laughed. "Whatever. The thing is, imagination or not, seeing Libby run out with a rain cloud chasing her will definitely top my list of treasured teen memories."

"Speaking of Libby, is she here yet?" From the corner of her eye, Sabrina saw Salem slip a can of smoked oysters under the can opener.

Val winced. "Yeah. She called Mr. Kraft this morning to cancel. Bad move. He drove over to pick her up. Libby's not a joy when she's happy, but she's totally impossible when she's mad."

"She is, isn't she? Let's go have a good time and make her madder." Sabrina glanced over her shoulder on her way out. "Give it up, Salem. All the appliances are on strike."

Salem stared at the can opener and whined pitifully. "Pretty please?"

In the dining room Mr. Kraft tried to snitch a shrimp while Hilda's back was turned. She slapped his hand away without turning to look.

"How do you do that?" Looking mildly handsome in his gray tux, Mr. Kraft scowled.

"You're a high school vice principal and you don't know?" Hilda scoffed.

"Eyes in the back of your head, huh?"

"Something like that." Hilda steered Val toward the kitchen, zapping the shrimp Mr. Kraft picked up as she walked away. He dropped the sizzling morsel and looked around guiltily.

"Come on, Willard. I want to show you where to stand." Aunt Zelda motioned from the doorway. "Sabrina, help Harvey at the door, will you?"

"Yes, ma'am!" Sabrina gave Zelda a thumbs-up as her aunt took Mr. Kraft's arm. Apparently, she and Hilda had agreed on a Willard truce for the duration of the wedding.

Sitting by herself, Libby nervously scanned the living room as though she expected to be struck by lightning any second. Sabrina walked straight to the foyer, opting to keep the peace instead of disrupting Aunt Vesta's happy event for a bit of satisfaction at Libby's expense. One night with the misery-cloud was more than enough payback for a while.

"Hi, Sabrina." Harvey smiled with relief and unabashed admiration. "You look beautiful."

"Thanks. You're look great, too."

Harvey scratched under his stiff collar. "I've never done this ushering thing before. I'm a little nervous."

"Don't be. Just escort the guests to the chairs and let them pick where they want to sit. Everyone in Aunt Vesta's family is already here, and we know where we belong." Sabrina paused. "That didn't come out right, did it?"

The doorbell rang.

"I'll get it." Taking a deep breath, Harvey stiffened and opened the door. "Welcome to the, uh— Spellman wedding."

"Relax, Harvey! You sound like a butler." Sabrina grinned when Ash and an older gentleman in a dark suit walked in. "Hey! The groom's here!"

"Hello, Sabrina." Ash gallantly kissed her hand.

"You look absolutely stunning today. This is Judge Wilcox. He's performing the ceremony."

"Oh, good." Harvey grinned. "You both stand up so I guess I don't have to seat you."

"My knees are shaking so hard, I may have to sit down before I fall down," Ash said, chuckling. Spotting Mr. Kraft, he guided Judge Wilcox into the living room.

"Hello?" Marla rapped on the doorjamb.

Harvey snapped to attention. "Welcome—"

"Hi, Marla! Come on in." Sabrina sighed inwardly as the shy associate professor stumbled over the threshold. Her dark hair hung limply to her shoulders under a beret she had pulled down over her ears. Yesterday's baggy brown sweater and plaid skirt had been exchanged for a baggy gray sweater and black skirt. "I'm so glad to see you again."

Marla nodded. "Could I use the rest room?"

"Sure. It's right up—wait. I've got to tell Aunt Vesta something. Just follow me. You're on your own, Harvey."

"Storming Gertrude's castle was a lot less terrifying," Harvey muttered.

Aunt Vesta was pacing in the upstairs hall. With her shining auburn hair drawn back in an elaborate twist, she looked ravishing in a gown she and Hilda had found at a bridal shop on Main Street. The skirt fell in soft folds that swished alluringly as she walked. Lace trimmed the scooped-neck bodice and cuffed the long sleeves. The ugly shawl hung from her arms and she clutched a bouquet of blue tea roses, white baby's breath, and lacy ferns. New, old, and blue were covered.

"Aunt Vesta!" Sabrina hissed. "Ash is here!"

Vesta nodded and smiled at Marla. "Hello, Marla."

"Hi, Vesta." Marla waved meekly and pulled a pearl necklace from a pocket in her skirt. "Uh, I thought you might want to wear this. Unless you already have something borrowed."

"Thank you, Marla. How sweet of you to think of it." Vesta took the offered pearls and gave them to Sabrina to clasp around her neck.

"Ash, I mean Professor Whittier, has always been kind to me. I just wanted to do something because—" Marla cleared a catch in her throat. "Because I'm so happy he's found someone he really loves. Someone who really loves him back, you know?"

"Yes, I think I do, Marla," Vesta said solemnly.

"Excuse me." Pushing her glasses back onto her nose, Marla headed down the hall.

"Wow," Sabrina whispered. "That was heavy."

"Ditto," Vesta said softly, casually flicking her finger as Marla turned into the bathroom.

Thunder boomed and lightning flashed in the linen closet.

Downstairs, Libby screamed.

"That must be Dad and Gail!" Sabrina winced. "Maybe I should have told them to come through the book in my room."

"They're here now. Too late!" Flashing a brilliant smile, Vesta ran to hug Ted as he emerged from the closet with Gail on his arm. "Hello, you little brat!"

"I see impending captivity hasn't dulled your spirit, Vesta." Ted Spellman laughed and a *ping* sparkled off his front tooth.

Gail rummaged in her purse and handed him a small tooth duller spray. "Put it in your pocket, Ted."

Ted ran over to Sabrina and kissed her on the cheek. "You look gorgeous. And I mean that, even if I am your father."

"Later, Dad. I've got to get back downstairs before Harvey's knees lock permanently. You wait up here with Aunt Vesta. Gail!" Sabrina waved. "You're with me!"

As Sabrina and Gail started down the stairs, thunder boomed and lightning cracked again.

Libby screamed.

Sabrina looked back and gasped as all the Spellman relatives from the Other Realm filed out of the linen closet.

Chapter 15

"This is *not* happening." Standing in the dining room doorway, Hilda gawked as the various members of their very strange family trooped down the stairs and took seats.

Chubby Cousin Mortimer strode in wearing his magician costume. He paused to let dour Cousin Doris walk down the aisle ahead of him.

"Aunt Vesta thought it was funny." Sabrina winced when Cousin Susie, who looked like a wicked, fairy-tale witch but had a heart of gold, introduced herself to a speechless Sadie and her flustered husband, Bernard.

"Funny?" Zelda started. "She's the one who didn't want to invite them in the first place!"

"I know." Sabrina shrugged. "She seemed kind of down until Dad got here. Then it was like a light suddenly went on, and she became her old, care-free, irrepressible self."

Salem rubbed against Sabrina's leg and sat down to survey the scene. "Well, well, well. Look what the linen closet dragged in."

Cousin Marigold hauled a petulant Amanda to a chair by the wall and ordered her to sit down. Amanda promptly zapped up a handheld TV and started to blow a bubble with Other Realm gum. Marigold zapped the gum away before the bubble popped and demolished every house in the neighborhood with a bang several magnitudes louder than a sonic boom.

"Wedding jitters," Hilda said, frowning. "I've never seen this many Spellmans together in one place before. Only five of us showed up at the last family reunion in 1742."

"That blank invitation I sent by mistake obviously didn't end up in the dead-letter file." Sabrina waved at Cousin Chris, who had dressed in a regular suit instead of the fur-trimmed red one he wore to make his rounds on Christmas Eve.

"Uh-oh." Zelda ducked back. "There's Cousin Larry. I hope he's not still mad at me for getting the best of him at our postwar summit. I insisted that he make my conquered population tax-exempt citizens."

"Cheapskate. There were only three of them." Hilda sighed. "He's sitting next to Great-granny. You could be in trouble."

"I don't see Boyd, Racine, and Maw Maw. Not that I want to—ever again," Sabrina clarified emphatically. They'd still be feuding with the hillbilly branch of the family if Great-granny hadn't intervened.

Hilda wrinkled her nose. "If Boyd and Racine can't get a message through jug-net, they don't want to know."

"It works on the same principal as jungle drums," Salem explained, "except a bunch of old guys blow on jugs."

"Helooooo!" Cousin Beulah's loud shrill voice sent dozens of hands up to cover dozens of ears.

"That's my cue to bail out." Salem yawned and walked away. "Call me when the reception starts. Think I'll grab a nap so I'm primed for some serious shrimp snitching later."

"Just stay off the buffet table!" Hilda warned the cat, then flinched when the vivacious and outrageous Beulah butted Crystal to move over. Crystal's husband, Stephen, stared straight ahead until Gail pulled Beulah into a chair on the bride's side of the room.

"Hold on to your credit cards. Cousin Zsa Zsa just came in." Sabrina sagged as a pert and pretty girl with *big* hair sat by Val. Zsa Zsa's magical wares never worked as advertised, and they did not come with a money-back guarantee. "If anyone buys something from her, we'll have to initiate major catastrophe control."

"What *are* we going to do?" Hilda asked Zelda.

"Hope for the best and if all else fails, zap up some truffles."

Sabrina's gaze was drawn to the foyer. None of the Spellman weirdness was as startling as the sight of Marla gliding down the aisle to take a front seat. She had lost the glasses and carried herself with poised confidence. A radiant smile lit up her face, and her dark hair fell in soft curls under a beret worn at a cocky angle. The sweater had shrunk to fit, and shimmering silver threads had been added to the gray knit. The baggy black skirt now flared dramatically at the hip.

So what happened since I saw her in the hall? Sabrina wondered, then remembered Aunt Vesta's casual point. Instant makeover.

When Ash realized that the woman walking toward him was Marla, he stumbled back against the fireplace. Mr. Kraft grabbed his arm to steady him. Judge Wilcox looked at his watch.

Harvey skirted the chairs along the front wall to reach the piano, where Libby was huddled with her tape recorder. Catching Sabrina's eye, he thumbed toward the stairs. Aunt Vesta was ready.

"One of you has to walk down the aisle with her," Sabrina reminded her other aunts.

Hilda and Zelda looked at each other and shrugged. They each put a hand behind their backs. "I'll call it," Hilda said. "Evens. One, two, three!"

"Three!" Zelda counted the total fingers they each held out. "Bye!"

Muttering under her breath, Hilda popped upstairs.

Zelda grabbed Sabrina's hand and they took seats in the back row behind Zsa Zsa and Val. Heaving a resigned sigh, Libby stepped forward and began singing when Harvey hit the Play button on the recorder.

"Something in the way she moves. . . ."

Everyone stood up and looked back as Hilda walked down the stairs with a fake smile firmly in place. Oohs and ahs rippled through the room as the bride came into view on Ted's arm. Val sniffled and dabbed her eyes with a paper napkin, and Sabrina crossed her fingers as they started down the aisle. Aunt Vesta had the awful black shawl draped around her shoulders, which sent a whisper of curiosity coursing from mortal to mortal. None of the other Spellman women were aware that their romantic fates were at stake. The secret of the spinster shawl had been entrusted to Vesta, a secret she had kept until she confided in Sabrina and her aunts.

But Vesta still didn't know how to break the spell.

Sabrina tensed as her father sat down and the bride and groom faced the judge with Hilda and Mr. Kraft flanking them. Harvey turned off the recorder and sat beside Libby in the front row. Annoyed, Sabrina forced her attention back to the ceremony when Judge Wilcox started speaking. Her hands were knotted into anxious fists by the time Mr. Kraft took a ring from his pocket. Val and Beulah sobbed as Ash turned to Vesta and took her hand.

"Do you, Ashton, take—"

"Wait." Vesta pulled her hand away. "I'm sorry, Ash. I can't do this. I can't explain, either, except to say—I care more than you'll ever know."

Sabrina stared in disbelief.

Ash paled as Vesta kissed him lightly, then ran back up the aisle. The black shawl fell off her shoulders and turned white before it settled on the floor.

☆

Chapter 16

☆

The stunned hush that had fallen over the room
ended abruptly when Vesta disappeared through
the dining room door. Nervous laughter punctu-
ated the buzz of conversation as the meaning of
Vesta's actions sank in.

"She just walks away?" Val threw up her hands.
"Just like that? Why?"

"I'm not sure, but I have my suspicions." Sabrina picked up the white shawl and handed it to
Zelda. Without a word, Zelda folded it and left to
go after her sister. Sabrina did a quick scan of the
room to access everyone else's reaction.

Up front, Ash started to move toward the dining
room. Hilda stopped him with a hand on his chest
and a shake of her head. As Marla led the stricken
groom to a chair, Mr. Kraft began to argue with
Hilda. Hilda's crossed arms and adamant expres-

sion left no doubt that the exercise was futile. Libby was making another play for Harvey. Sabrina checked an impulse to interfere. She hadn't had an opportunity to prove she really did trust him since the class marriage fiasco. *No time like the present.*

The guests on both sides of the aisle were standing up and starting to mingle, asking questions and offering opinions. Apparently, the Spellmans' odd appearances and eccentric natures were easily overlooked in the aftermath of the bride's unexpected announcement and exit.

"Take charge of things out here for me, will you, Val? Try to keep everyone calm. Just until I find out what's going on?"

Val glanced at the crowd, then looked at Sabrina askance. "This is a riot in the making. What if they start taking sides when the shock wears off?"

"Throw on a CD and feed them!" Sabrina pushed through the throng and edged around Cousin Mortimer and Sadie on her way to the kitchen.

"Vesta always was unpredictable." Mortimer flipped his black magician's cape over his shoulder.

"She seemed like such a refined and steady young woman, too." Sadie sighed.

"Vesta?" Mortimer burst out laughing. He laughed so hard that paper flowers sprouted from his top hat, pockets, and coat sleeves and a dove flew out of his cane.

"Oh, my." Sadie blinked, then applauded. "Do you know any more tricks?"

Wonderful, Sabrina thought as she pushed through the kitchen door. Cousin Mortimer couldn't resist an audience or the temptation to use real magic to cover his bumbled mortal tricks. That, however, hardly seemed important when Sabrina saw Vesta sitting at the table, wiping tears from her eyes with the shawl and looking totally devastated. Sabrina quietly slid into a chair.

Hilda barged through the door in a huff. "Did I miss the explanation? I hope not because I can't wait to hear it."

Aunt Zelda zapped up a box of tissues. She gave one to Vesta in exchange for the shawl, which she tossed to Hilda.

"This isn't—" Hilda faltered. "Is it?"

Sabrina nodded. "The shawl changed color after Aunt Vesta—you know."

"Dumped the perfect man at the altar?" Hilda quipped.

Salem was asleep in his usual spot on the counter. His eyes popped open. "Does that mean the reception is canceled?"

"Forget the reception!" Hilda examined the shawl more closely. "It's not just white. It looks brand-new. Does this mean—"

"That the spinster curse is no longer in effect?" Zelda finished. "I think so, yes."

"Cool!" Hilda brightened. "When did you figure out how to break the spell, Vesta?"

"I didn't." Vesta blew her nose, then dried her

eyes with another tissue. "The spell wasn't the reason I decided not to marry Ash."

Sabrina sat back. "It's not? Then why? I mean, you're obviously very much in love with him."

"That's why." Composing herself, Vesta pointed a cup of herbal tea and took a sip. "When I was standing up there, I realized that I loved him too much to live a lie and that I couldn't live without magic. I couldn't risk telling him I'm a witch, and he deserves someone he can trust. Someone who'd put his happiness before her own."

Sabrina didn't doubt Vesta's motives, but she was sure there was more to it. She had told her aunt that Gertrude wanted her to give Harvey to Libby. That was the perfect revenge considering that Gertrude had lost her true love, Cornelius, to their great-grandmother, Daphne. Vesta had figured out that giving up *her* true love to another was the only way to break the spinster spell.

"Someone like Marla?" Sabrina asked gently. "I know what you did for her."

"Then that part worked well," Hilda muttered. "She's consoling Ash as we speak."

Vesta grinned mischievously. "I just altered her clothes, styled her hair and gave her contacts. That's all it took to coax the *real* Marla out of her shell."

"Oh, dear." Zelda's eyes widened slightly. "We're not cursed without knowing it anymore."

"And the problem with that is—" Hilda asked sarcastically.

"Nothing." Zelda shrugged. "I just hope Willard isn't thinking about popping the question. He's sweet, but I'm not ready to settle down yet."

"I'll sleep better knowing that." Hilda's scowl shifted to a smile of sudden revelation. "Hey! Maybe the next time I'm dating a guy who adores me, the relationship won't end because he thinks I'm dead!"

"And Harvey and I have a future together!" Sabrina jumped up. "Maybe. After college. I gotta go!"

"Me, too." Vesta rose with a flamboyant flourish of her hand that cleared her reddened eyes and repaired her smudged makeup. "Suddenly I feel like a party!"

"Now you're talking!" Salem leaped off the counter into Vesta's arms. "Take me to your shrimp platter!"

Sabrina and her aunts burst back into the dining room to find the party was already in full swing. Mr. Kraft was piling shrimp onto a plate, unaware that Amanda was under the table tying his shoelaces together. The chairs had been stacked against the walls in the living room, and several mismatched couples were dancing to the rocking beat of an oldies CD. Beulah was teaching Bernie the rump bump, and Val struggled to follow as Emperor Larry waltzed her around the floor. Dour Cousin Doris and Cousin Chris held each other at arm's length doing the box step Sabrina had learned in junior high. Her father and Gail held each other close as they swayed from side to side without moving their feet.

In the corner by the foyer Cousin Mortimer entertained an enthralled Sadie with his amazing feats of magic. Ash and Marla were sitting on the piano bench, holding hands and talking. Cousin Sally dragged Cousin Zsa Zsa away from Stephen, who was reaching for his wallet. Cousin Marigold was looking for Amanda.

"Come on, Salem," Vesta said. "I'll fix you a plate."

"A plate! You mean I don't have to snitch and run for the nearest dark corner?" The cat purred in her arms. "How long were you planning to stay?"

"Looks like everyone's having a good time." Hilda glanced sideways at Zelda. "Wanna shoot fingers for the first dance with Willard? We seem to have a shortage of available men."

Zelda grinned. "If you can get him away from the shrimp, he's all yours. For one dance."

Realizing that Harvey and Libby were both absent, Sabrina wandered into the living room. She peeked into the foyer. They weren't there. *Trust,* she reminded herself as she looked in the den and didn't find them there, either. It took all her willpower, but she refrained from conducting a thorough search of the whole house. Feeling awkward and alone, she stood behind Sadie and absently watched Mortimer's magic show.

"This is very difficult." Wiggling his fingers to loosen up, Cousin Mortimer removed his top hat and set it on a chair. "I'm sure I'll get it right this time."

"You're doing just wonderfully, Mortimer." Sadie smiled to encourage him. "I've never seen anyone make the printing on a whole deck of cards vanish before."

"You're so sweet. Okay. Here goes." He closed his eyes.

"Have either of you seen Harvey?" Sabrina asked.

"That handsome young usher?" Sadie nodded. "He left with the singer a little while ago."

"Oh. Thanks." Sabrina smiled tightly. Harvey had a good reason for leaving with Libby. She was sure he had a good reason.

"Are you finished, Sabrina? I have to concentrate." When she nodded, Mortimer closed his eyes and held his cane over the hat.

*"Fire and dirt, wind and rain,
Make my rabbit come back again!"*

Mortimer waved the cane and tapped the hat.

And the misery-cloud *whooshed* out to hover over his head.

"Hey, little drip!" Sabrina laughed. "Welcome back!"

The misery-cloud rumbled.

"You know this cloud?" Mortimer was mortified. "I didn't conjure a cloud. I wanted my rabbit!"

"Don't be upset, dear. It's a darling cloud." Sadie stood up and patted Mortimer's arm. "Wait here. I'll get you some punch. You'll feel better."

The front door slammed.

Sabrina whirled and smiled as Harvey walked toward her with a sheepish grin.

"Sorry I had to leave. Libby wanted to go home like right *now* and Mr. Kraft wouldn't take her. So I gave her a ride."

"That was so sweet of you. Wanna dance?"

"Yeah! I'd love to."

Mortimer sobbed and the misery-cloud drizzled.

Harvey didn't notice as he took Sabrina in his arms and swept her onto the dance floor. He only had eyes for her.

About the Author

Diana G. Gallagher lives in Minnesota with her husband, Marty Burke, three dogs, three cats, a cranky parrot, and a guinea pig called Red Alert. When she's not writing, she spends her time walking the dogs, puttering in the yard, playing the guitar, and going to garage sales looking for cool stuff for her grandsons, Jonathan, Alan, and Joseph.

A Hugo Award–winning artist, Diana is best known for her series *Woof: The House Dragon.* Dedicated to the development of the solar system's resources, she has contributed to this effort by writing and recording songs that promote and encourage humanity's movement into space. She also loves Irish and folk music and performs at local coffeehouses and science-fiction conventions around the country.

Her first adult novel, *The Alien Dark,* appeared in 1990. She and Marty coauthored *The Chance Factor,* a *Starfleet Academy Voyager* book. In addition to other *Star Trek* novels for intermediate readers, Diana has written many books in other series published by Minstrel Books, including *The Secret World of Alex Mack, Are You Afraid of the Dark,* and *The Mystery Files of Shelby Woo.* She is currently working on original young adult novels for the Archway Paperback series *Sabrina the Teenage Witch* and the Pocket Books series of *Buffy the Vampire Slayer* novels.

DON'T MISS ANY OF OUR
BEST-SELLING POP MUSIC BIOS!

Backstreet Boys ☆ Aaron Carter
by Matt Netter

Five
by Matt Netter

Dancin' With Hanson
by Ravi

Hanson: Mmmbop to the Top
by Jill Matthews

Isaac Hanson: Totally Ike!
by Nancy Krulik

Taylor Hanson: Totally Taylor!
by Nancy Krulik

Zac Hanson: Totally Zac!
by Matt Netter

Hanson: The Ultimate Trivia Book
by Matt Netter

Jewel: Pieces of a Dream
by Kristen Kemp

Pop Quiz
by Nancy Krulik

'N Sync: Tearin' Up the Charts
by Matt Netter

Will Smith: Will Power!
by Jan Berenson

ROSWELL HIGH

He's not like other guys.

Liz has seen him around. It's hard to miss Max—the tall, blond, blue-eyed senior stands out in her high-school crowd. So why is he such a loner?

Max is in love with Liz. He loves the way her eyes light up when she laughs. And the way her long, black hair moves when she turns her head. Most of all, he loves to imagine what it would be like to kiss her.

But Max knows he can't get too close. He can't let her discover the truth about who he is. Or really, what he is....Because the truth could kill her.

One astounding secret...a shared moment of danger...life will never be the same.

A new series by Melinda Metz

**Available from Archway Paperbacks
Published by Pocket Books**

2034